Caribbean Twilight: Tales of the Supernatural

By Clyde Viechweg

Caribbean Twilight: Tales of the Supernatural by Clyde Viechweg

For info, contact: Caribbeantwilight@gmail.com

Cover Design by: LLPIX Photography. LLPIX.com
Edited by: Hercules Editing and Consulting Services. BZHercules.com

This book is dedicated these most special people in my life:

Malikah Bain, Mikaeli Bain, Alexei Campbel, Vilma Cenac, Arthur Viechweg

Special thanks to:

Charissa Cenac, Kayla Cenac, Byron Campbel , Clarice Cenac, Natalie Aisha Charles, Andrea Viechweg, William Cenac, Irene Cenac, Sharie Mc Cool , Safiya Sawney, Herbert Williams, and to all my Facebook friends.

Clyde Viechweg

Introduction

I was raised on the island of Grenada with an abundance of folklore and tall tales on rainy or full moon evenings.

I found them frighteningly entertaining and delighted in the way the various storytellers delivered their narrations. You could not help but to look in the closet and under your bed before sleeping.

Today, things have changed, and I fear these tales that are rooted in our Caribbean tradition might soon be lost forever.

So, I have undertaken a rather ambitious plan to keep them alive and well in the hearts and minds of future generations.

Even if you may not be from the Caribbean, you may find some similarities between them and your own culture, and to this end, I have aimed at finding common ground among the diverse cultures of the world, one story at a time.

Clyde Viechweg, "Storyteller"

Clyde Viechweg

Caribbean Twilight: Tales of the Supernatural

Clyde Viechweg

The La Diablesse

I remember it like it was yesterday.

It was a beautiful full moon night, under a Caribbean sky. The sky was clear and bright with the silver reflection of the moon everywhere. I was attending a house party in Grenville. It turned out to be quite boring, and at around 12:30 a.m., I told my host I was leaving.

"Clyde it is so late. Why don't you spend the night and leave in the morning?"

I politely declined the offer, citing that I had obligations later that morning. The truth was that I was disappointed that there were no single ladies at the party.

I headed out for the town of St. Georges, driving over the Grand Etang Mountains. As I accelerated, I could feel the power in the car as it pushed me back against the seat. The corners came fast and it was proving to be the highlight of my evening. In ten minutes, I made quick work of the hills while rocking to the music of DMX. At the bottom of the mountain lies a bridge before you enter Vendome village. As I approached the bridge, I saw a woman sitting on one of the walls. I slowed down as I came closer, wondering, *What is this lady doing out here with her cute self?*

I pulled up next to her and said, "Hey, pretty, are you okay? What are you doing out here at this ungodly hour? Would you like a ride somewhere?" My first two questions brought no response from her. I concluded that she probably had a fight with her boyfriend and he had left her there. However, my offer of the ride brought a huge smile to her face. It was there I noticed her eyes—shining and reflecting the moon light. There was almost a hypnotic effect. I felt myself being drawn into them. Something inside of me pulled me back. That something was a sense of danger that not all was well here. Anyway, I brushed the feeling off and asked, "Would you like the ride or not?"

She shook her head, signaling "yes," got up, and began making her way to the car. I expected her to cross in front of the car so that I could get a good look at her, but she walked to the back of the car instead. Now, the car is a two-door, so she had to come around to the front.

As she walked past me, I noticed that her dress reached all the way to the road. I also noticed that the dress was one you would wear to church. I felt that sense of danger in my stomach again, this time stronger. I looked in the side mirror as she passed me. There was no reflection of her body!!! I floored the accelerator and took off like a bat out of hell.

I heard a screeching laughter in the background. "Haha haaaaaa aaha!"

I made it home in less than ten minutes; to me it felt like two. In my yard, I turned off the engine breathed a sigh of relief. I found myself trembling and thinking, *What the hell just happened?* I was about to open the door when I turned around and saw her sitting in the back seat. I tried to scream, but no sound came out, and her face transformed into a hideous mask. Her eyes locked in on mine and I started falling into an endless pit. At that moment, I uttered a prayer that arose in my mind and the hold was broken. Her face returned to normal and she said to me, "Be careful; not everything that glitters is gold!" With that, she vanished into that slivery night.

10

Tales of a Ligaroo

Somewhere out there in the vast turquoise blue Caribbean Sea, to its west, and the turbulent Atlantic Ocean, to its east, lays a gem of an island. For those who are nautically savvy, the coordinates are 12 degrees 03 ' N 61 degrees 45 'W. And, if like Christopher Columbus, you hear her siren song and you feel yourself being drawn to her shores, resist not; for at the end of that tug is the tropical island paradise of Grenada.

To the northwest of the capital St. Georges, lays a quaint and beautiful village called Mt. Moritz. It is here my story begins, among the backdrop of fertile, cultivated valleys of mangos, oranges, golden apples, and every sort of godly fruit. Today, if its original Scottish settlers were to come back, they would notice a distinctive change. Long gone is the ravine flowing with water, teeming with fish and crayfish. The tiny homes are now replaced by stately houses and shops; streetlights are everywhere. The Internet and cell phones would certainly astonish them. However, through all this change, they would soon feel at home, for the fertile soil and the character of the inhabitants remain untouched.

In the time of my childhood, power outage was quite commonplace. Now for those of you who grew up on the island, this became part of life. You noticed it as much as you would pay attention to a sunset.

What you did notice was the black and blue bruises to the ladies' thighs and their complaints of a Ligaroo's indiscretions. Those tales brought fear to the little ones at night. I would find myself peeking out the window, looking for that infamous ball of fire.

Now, as it always happens, a rumor soon begins circulating of who the culprit is. In this case, it was Papa Geedo. When I heard this rumor, it was easy to believe, for Papa Geedo was a strange man who kept strange times and no company. He

11

resided in a little wooden house in the back of the Bocus. When he was seen in the village, he always wore a black felt hat, with black pants and shirt. His eyes always seemed to be bloodshot red.

My best friend at the time, I will call "Sam" to protect the identity of the individual. Sam and I, being adventurous youth, decided to get to the bottom of this rumor. So we started asking people about how a Ligaroo operated. Our most reliable source turned out to be my grandma. She said, "Ligaroos came from Africa with the slaves; they were Obeah men who drank blood to satisfy their deity." She continued, "They come out when the moon is full for three days, in search of a healthy victim."

"What can be done to stop one?" I asked.

"They can be stopped by following them and salting their skin, for they must shed their skin to take the form of a Ligaroo."

So it was then and there that Sam and I hatched our plan to rid the Mt. Moritz of a Ligaroo. Two days before the full moon, Sam went to the church and got a bottle of holy water and I stole a pound of salt from my house. We were reckless youth who thought Ligaroos were old wives' tales. I could hardly contain myself from excitement.

The day of the full moon was upon us. At 10 p.m., Sam and I took up our positions outside of Papa Geedo's house and waited. We tried our best to stop giggling as we speculated on the outcome of this adventure. Looking back on this moment, we never expected anything to come out of it, for we did not believe in such crap.

At 11:30 p.m., Papa Geedo came out the door. Something seemed different about him; he seemed to move with the ease of someone filled with energy and vigor. He started making his way out of the Bocus. We followed as stealthily as possible. At the main road in Mt. Moritz, he turned right, heading up the road. We continued following him all the way past the last house in upper Mt. Moritz until he finally stopped in front of a huge silk cotton tree.

What happened next changed the lives of two reckless youth forever, for after that night our view of life shifted drastically. Papa Geedo walked up to the trunk of the tree, looked around

12

him quickly, and then he proceeded to strip down naked. Sam and I now started getting nervous. This was not as funny as we had imagined earlier.

Standing naked under the tree while Sam and I hid behind a tree on our stomachs, Papa Geedo proceeded to stand on one leg while staring at the moon. He then started reciting an incantation that went something like this. *"Blue snake, black snake bring Papa Geedo a blood cake, cover him with an invisible cape."*

This incantation was kept up for twenty minutes. Suddenly the ground started shaking, and a huge black snake came out of a hole in the tree. The snake glowed, its eyes red as fire. It slithered over to Papa Geedo and breathed what appeared to be a mist onto him. In that moment, Papa Geedo collapsed on the ground. A huge ball of fire soon stood where the snake and Papa Geedo was last standing. The ball of fire shot off into the night sky, heading down into the village.

I could hear Sam's teeth clattering, or was it mine? Who knows; who cares? Five minutes later, we pulled ourselves together and approached the spot where the ball of fire was last seen. In its place was a mass of slimy skin. Sam threw the holy water and I threw the salt onto the skin. A loud hissing sound came out of nowhere and we took off running . . .and, boy, did we run! We ran straight through the front door without opening it. This woke everyone up. We related our tale and we were rewarded with a sound beating for staying out this late and for concocting tall tales.

Needless to say, Papa Geedo was never seen again. The villagers were heard murmuring that he probably moved to his family in the country. Sam and I never discussed that night again. However, the two of us were soon avid churchgoers.

I hope I have not frightened you off going to Mt. Moritz. Long gone are the days of the Ligaroo and Papa Geedo. The silk cotton tree still stands there as a witness to the supernatural.

If you ever find yourself on the isle of Spice, don't forget to look up in the sky on a full moon night, for Papa Geedo in flight.

John and the Sea Devil

In life, there are two kinds of intelligence: one is found in books and school; the other in experience and observation, commonly called common sense. For most of us, nature and environment dictate the allotments we each receive. Rare indeed are those who have both in abundance. Instead, we are given more in one or the other and finding the balance is in our hands.

As to which intelligence John was allotted, I will let you, the reader, form your own conclusions at the end of the story.

John was born in the village of Gand Mall, in the parish of St. Georges, Grenada. He was the last of six children: three girls and two boys ahead of him. John's father was a tailor by trade and his mother was a fish vendor. Gand Mall is a scenic fishing village along the northwest coast of St. Georges that is divided in two by the main highway that circles the island. The village has sweeping vistas of the blue Caribbean Sea and two amazing white, sandy beaches. It is here also that Shell Gas and Texaco Gas have their depots. The land above the road is scattered with houses that take advantage of the ocean views. On the other side of the road, there are few houses due to less space; however, they are only a stone's throw from the ocean.

John's future was shaped in large part by being born so close to the ocean and having a mother who vended fish. For being the last, he was always with his mother. In fact, he attended school as much as the devil would have attended church. So it was unfortunate that John never learned to read or write. However, with the case of most people in that circumstance, he quickly adapted to his environment and was soon a skillful fisherman by the age of sixteen.

His desire for money separated John from his peers. And, boy, did he know money! John could close his eyes and, by touch alone, he could tell which currency denomination was in his palm. He worked tirelessly six days of the week; neither did he touch spirits of any kind and he saved whatever little money he made. Truth be told, fishing has less to do with skill than luck. For one can read the tides and weather, but if the fish are not biting, your skill is in vain.

John had everything except luck. For the six days he fished, he barely caught much, so life was not easy for him. His father begged him to become his apprentice, but John refused, for the ocean was his calling no matter how cruel she was to him.

"One day, one day, my luck must change," he would say. Never would he let anything negative change his course.

It was 4 a.m. Friday morning. John made his way to his boat, walking along the dirt trail while the moon lighted his path. The air was fresh and filled with negatively charged ions from the sea. His body filled quickly with energy and a relaxed feeling swept over him.

Besides him, there were only a few crabs about their business. As he walked past houses, dogs would bark and feign attack. However, he paid them no mind. He made out the faint scent of coco tea and fry fish drifting in the trade winds. This he knew were the fishermen's wives preparing lunch for their husbands' day at sea.

Today, John felt lucky. He got to his boat, loaded his gear, and put out to sea. This morning, the sea was serene and his boat, *Lady D*, sliced through the water as a knife through butter.

There is something to being on water that calms the mind. Maybe because we spent nine months in a water bag in our mother's womb, thought John. *That was the safest place, for out in the world is a dark and cold place...maybe our whole life is to seek a safety net like our mother's on Earth,* he reasoned.

His meditation was soon broken by the splashing of flying fish. He pulled back on the throttle, bringing the boat to a standstill. John sprung into action. He pounded some sprat and threw them into the water, which attracted the flying fish. His net followed and soon he was hauling in bales of fish. When he had enough flying fish to bait his hooks, he stopped and started prepping his long line for tuna. Tuna is where the money is in fishing and today was John's lucky day after all. Or was it?

With his 30 hooks baited and set, all that was left to do was relax and wait for the tuna to bite. And bite they did! The buoys were dragged down and John leapt into action. He tried to start the boat, but it did not respond. He tried and tried and nothing happened except that the *Lady D* was drifting away from his lines fast. John pounded his hands on the motors, but that yielded no response. When he looked up, his buoys were nowhere to be seen.

Now it's one thing not catch any fish, but to lose one's long line was to invite ruin. Despair soon overwhelmed John; all his failures and negative thoughts came rushing in. He knew this was the end, for he would not be able to afford another line even if he got rescued. Tears flowed freely down his face.

"Why me, why me," he cried. "I am an honest man. I work hard and I am kind to the unfortunate. Why me, Lord? Why me? Ahha haaah aah, I would give my soul away for a chance to find my lines and go home!" he shouted between sobs.

"You would really give your soul for those things?" a voice spoke behind him. John spun around in terror. Standing behind him was a half-naked man, his lower part of his body submerged.

"Who is you, who is you?" screamed John. "Oh god ooh, doh' kill me, ah doh' want to deading!" cried John.

The half-naked man smiled at John, who had curled up in a ball with his eyes closed. "John, I am not going to kill you," said he.

"Mameee, oh god, ah deading now, how yuh know mi name, whoay ah deading!" screamed John.

The half-naked man waited until John stopped crying. "John, I want to help you get back home with all the fish on your line too. Also, I have been watching you for years and know that you're a hard worker and that you need a change of luck. John, I will do all these things for you in exchange for one little promise from you," said he.

John opened his eyes and looked at the man. He seemed so polite and he reminded him of his mother in some strange way. "Sir, what yuh want me to promise?"

"John, for the next twenty years, I would bless you in everything in exchange for your soul," said he.

17

John considered his situation and realized that without the help of the half-naked man, he would most likely die at sea and besides, without his lines, he would not be able to fish and that was as good a death sentence as any. Besides, what was in a promise anyway? He had broken countless over the years with no seen consequences.

I can always milk our agreement for eighteen of the twenty years and not go to sea again, thought John.

All through his deliberation, the half-naked man observed John with a knowing smile. "Have you made up your mind?" he asked John.

"Yes, sir, I accept the deal." The half-naked man sprang onto John and pulled a piece of his hair from his head. John's heart went down into his toe and back.

"John, twenty years from today, I will come for you as promised. Now start your engines, and your lines are over there." John turned and was startled to see the boat on top of the lines. When he turned around, the man was gone.

Somehow, it felt like a bad dream. He tried the engines and they started smoothly. He then went about hauling in his catch and, to his amazement, 30 tuna was his take. Overjoyed, he headed for home, quickly forgetting his encounter. Needless to say, John was the toast of the village. He made so much money from that one catch, he stayed home a week, fêting the village.

Over the next twenty years, all John's dreams came true. He built a fleet of fishing boats, three houses, two shops, and yes, he even found love. John married the village beauty and fathered three loving kids. Life was good for an unlettered son of the soil who rose from a lowly station to great heights. Week after week, his boats came in, filled with fish, even when no other boats were catching anything. The villagers all said that God was with John; for they recalled how hard he worked as a youth and how much bad luck he faced early on in his career. They were truly happy for him, for in his prosperity he kept his kind heart and door opened to the needy.

So it was on that fateful day, exactly 20 years from the pact with the half-naked man that John put out to sea. Twenty years is a long time and time dims the memory. John had not been to sea in five years, but this morning, a desire consumed him to go fishing. It felt so good too. So John had a big breakfast of a dozen boiled eggs and told his wife he was going fishing.

"That's a great idea. You have been somewhat restless this past week and it should do you some good," said she. John smiled. However, he felt strange for she never wanted him fishing after the last child was born. However, he never bothered to seek the cause.

John guided the boat up the coast while drinking his favorite juice: passion fruit and lime. A shiny object soon caught his attention and he turned the boat towards it. As he pulled alongside it, the engines died. His stomach growled with gas from the eggs and juice. He turned towards the engines and lo and behold, the half-naked man was there. Everything came crashing back. John had forgotten his pact. Today, the half-naked man was looking far from friendly and pleasant as in their former meeting. His eyes were black and two little horns were jutting out the side of his forehead. His nails, or should I say claws, were long, black, and sharp. He was smiling and his teeth/fangs were yellow. "John, are you ready to pay up?"

"Oh God, no please no, I have kids, my wife, please have mercy!" cried John.

"God and mercy is in heaven and you are not heading there," said he.

"I am a good man, I helped people, I shared the wealth. Please, sir, please, have mercy on poor John!" pleaded John.

The creature looked at John with amusement, basking in poor John's torment. John's stomach growled even louder with gas.

"Okay, I am willing to let you go if you can come up with one task that I cannot perform within the ocean," said the Sea Devil to John, knowing that he was master of the sea.

By now, John was shaking in terror and he was in no shape for thinking, when suddenly he pummed (farted) and John pummed again and again. He turned to the devil and said, "Mr. Devil, write your name on that!"

19

The devil flew into a rage, but he could not break his word. He disappeared into the ocean. John cranked up the engines and headed home.

John never went back to sea again; he sold all his boats too. He eats a dozen boiled eggs every day still in case the devil was to show up again and a couple of hot pums on standby for the devil to sign his name.

Exorcism in Grenada

Forty years have elapsed, yet time has done little to erase the spiritual scar on my soul that was inflicted on me in the Year of Our Lord, 1969, in the village of La Digue, St. Andrews, Grenada.

My name is Father George Baker and this is my testimony. I leave to all the unbelievers of devils and demons and of all that walk in the ungodly craft of Satan.

I was born in Nottingham England, January 13th 1927 AD, to Lord Barry and Lady Ann Baker. I was the third of three children. My sister Catherine was the first, followed by Bancroft. My childhood was full of love and joy for Mother and Father doted over us at every opportunity. We lived off Alferton Road in an imposing estate home that was rightly called "The Hallows."

My mother was deeply religious and we attended service every Sunday at the Anglican Church rain or shine. The bishop who presided over the service was a frequent guest to our home for Sunday lunch. Bishop Samuel was a jolly 80-year-old man who would narrate biblical tales in the most elaborate and animated way, so that all witnesses were held captive under his spell. I loved the stories of the Bible. I imagined myself as David slaying Goliath and of Moses leading his people out of Egypt and crossing the Red Sea. The Bible was an enchanting world for a young dreamer such as myself. I made up my mind that I too would become a priest.

I graduated secondary school at the top of my class after some delay due to World War Two. I then went on to Oxford University to major in Classics. It was there again that the urge arose in me to become a man of the cloth. In my studies, I noticed similarities in Greek mythology and the Bible. There were good and bad forces, demigods, and God. Homer's Odyssey was a good analogy to the Israelites in the wilderness. Homer used the idea of spiritual growth as one of his underlying themes. This was a message that he related through various characters.

I graduated in 1957 and decided to attend Seminary College on the island of Barbados in the West Indies. I, having read much tales of pirates' adventures in the Caribbean in my youth, was thrilled at the prospect on studying there.

I arrived on the island of Barbados in 1958 to attend Codrington College to study Theology. The school was established in 1745 in the parish of St. John and taught Classics and Theology. I will not bore you with the details of school here, but I will fast forward to my ordination as a priest.

As a priest, I was sent to fill a vacancy at the Anglican Church in La Digue, St. Andrews, Grenada. I arrived on the island in 1968 and found it immediately charming. I moved into the rectory, which sat on a well-manicured lawn with flowers to either side of the house and a huge bamboo field to the front right. To the back of the house was cocoa. The church sat 60 feet away and it was made artfully out of stone. To say that it was quaint and unique would be to underscore its charm.

The church's cemetery lay between the Holy Innocent School and the church. I settled into my duties with ease, for the people were warm and friendly. Wherever I went in the village, I was received graciously and respectfully. I could not have imagined the village and my world would soon be turned upside down.

It came a year after my arrival. At ten o'clock, I heard a pounding at my door, so I slipped on my robe and made my way down the stairs to the door.

"Farda George, come quick. Spirit take Cece daughter. Come Farda come," he said while tugging at one of my sleeves. To say the least, I did not know whether to be amused or irritated at this intrusion, but somehow the urgency in his voice compelled me to follow him.

Cece's house was eleven houses down the street. As we approached the house, I noticed the yard was filled with people and was lit by two bottle torches. "Luk, luk, Farda coming!" Murmuring broke out. They cleared the way for me to enter the house. Inside, I was greeted by Cece, who was in a disheveled state, sobbing nonstop.

"Where is the child?" I asked. She pointed to the little room on the left. I walked into the room and I was jolted by the sight that greeted me! There on the bed was Cece's little daughter, who was thirteen years old, held down by two muscular men, yet they were barely holding on to the 100 lb child. Her face was distorted, while her eyes bulged outwards. Veins as large as snakes were popping up on her neck and froth was gushing out of her mouth. To say I was taken back was to simplify. I was paralyzed with fear and astonishment. We were taught about this in seminary school, but to actually witness this is as different as east is from west.

Cece's touch on my shoulder brought me out of my shock. I gathered whatever little wits I had left and moved into action. I ran home to retrieve my crucifix, Bible, and holy water, all the while praying.

Back at Cece's house, I found the men sweating profusely with labored breathing. The room was lit with two kerosene lanterns, which made the experience surreal. I asked for the room to be cleared with the exception of the two guys who were trying their utmost to hold her down. As soon I closed the door behind me, calmness entered the room. She stopped struggling. Instead, she followed my movement with only her eyes, with her lips curled up into a hideous grin.

"He that dwelleth in the secret place of the most high shall abide under the shadow of the almighty." I started reciting the 91st Psalm.

All hell broke loose. Pots and pans went flying, while rocks fell onto the roof from nowhere. Windows and doors opened and closed on their own. Stomping of feet was heard on the roof and ghastly sounds came out of her stomach. I threw the holy water on her. Steam rose from wherever the water landed on her. A strong sulfur scent mixed with rotting garage took over the room. The two guys were holding on for dear life.

I then placed the crucifix on her bosom and suddenly a deep voice addressed me. "George, George know ye not your place."

"Who are you?" I asked.

"I am Balma, demon prince of Grenada."

"Why do you possess this child?" I demanded.

23

"This child is going to grow up to bring many to the Lord. For this, she must die."

I continued reciting Psalm 91 and sprinkling holy water over her. For seven hours, we battled. The demon, being a prince, was strong. The bed was lifted off the floor with the three of them on the bed. But I persisted in supplication to God in prayer, asking that he send an angel to assist me. Suddenly, there appeared a glow in the room that moved towards the bed.

The demon screamed, "Gabriel, this concerns you not! Leave me in peace; our time is not yet come!" The light then faded into the girl's stomach. Convulsions soon followed with growling and obscenities and the whole house shook like it was caught in a hurricane. A huge black snake busted through the girl's stomach; it was covered in scales and slime. It shrieked and smashed through the roof and was gone. The girl stopped struggling and all was quiet. The two guys who were holding the girl down were dead, their heads ripped off. The girl opened her eyes. Seeing me, she said, "Father George, what are you doing here?"

"My child, my child!" I cried and hugged her tightly so she would not witness the dead men.

The sun was up when I left the house that morning; one life was saved and two were sacrificed in her place. There was wailing from the family for the two dead men and anger towards Cece.

Two weeks later, I arranged for Cece and her daughter to move to England, for they became pariahs in the village.

I hope this testimony will bring light to all who read this, for on the edge of this world, they are waiting: dark, powerful forces to sweep man off this Earth and to feed on his soul forever in darkness.

~Father George Baker, Archbishop of Canterbury, Head of the Church of England

The Baku

Nonpareil Village is located in St. Marks Parish. It sits comfortably between Waltham to the south and Industry to the north. Nonpareil enjoys cool ocean breezes off Crayfish Bay. Turning our heads east of the village, we can see Duquesne and Diego Piece Villages.

In the center of the village lies a burnt concrete structure of an impressive size, in contrast to dwellings in the rest of the village. The walls are black with soot, and there are grasses and moss growing throughout the imposing structure. Its only inhabitants now are birds, mice, and ants. If you're like me, you are probably wondering what brought about its fate.

That building that now lies in ruin was once a beautiful piece of architecture and even had a name too. It was called "Blue Diamond" and it was comprised of a discothèque and bar that carried every alcoholic drink imaginable in its inventory. The dance floor would accommodate 600 souls every Friday and Saturday night. The sound system would boom out the latest calypso, soca, reggae, and dancehall tunes. The gyrating bodies would move to its every beat, while dim red and soft blue mood lights would bathe the revelers.

At the back of the discothèque was a grocery and rum shop that opened seven days a week. Villagers would sit drinking and slamming dominos into the wee hours of the morning, to the annoyance of their spouses.

Above the discothèque and shop was the residence of the owner. The house had large glass windows that took advantage of the picturesque bay and mountain vistas. The floor was tiled in white, which matched the curtains. There were four bedrooms, three bathrooms, a kitchen, dining room, study, laundry, and theater room. Crystal, glass, and ceramic ornaments were displayed elegantly throughout the dwelling.

The master bedroom opened out onto a balcony that formed an L shape, so that both mountain and ocean views were

25

merged. Yes, life was good to Pompey. Did fortune always favor him? Let's us go back into the past and take a peek.

Pompey was born to Andrew and Betty Davis. He was their only child. Pompey's father was a farmer who worked hard to make his family as comfortable as crop prices would allow. Yams, dasheen, calliou, peas, cabbage, carrots, okra, seasoning peppers, and sorrel were what he cultivated. Betty stayed at home and cooked and cleaned, and when harvest time came, assisted her husband. They lived modestly and were quite content with their means.

Pompey, however, grew up always wanting more. In school, he excelled in all his disciplines. He graduated in the top three of his class. In a hurry to make his way in the world, he forewent further education and chose to pursue work. Pompey found work at American Airlines and looked forward to his bright future.

Soon, he was traveling abroad, meeting new people, and experiencing other cultures that he had only read about or had seen on television. In the village, he was looked upon with respect, and his parents were so proud.

However, soon he found himself spending more than he was making. Pompey loved the good life; the ladies even more. Eventually, he started borrowing money from his poor parents to support his reckless lifestyle. Since he was their only son, they gave whatever they could. It pricked his conscience to have to take money from his poor parents who labored so hard, so that he would not have to go through what they went.

As fate would have it, he was coming from the river and ran into Mother Lucy. Mother Lucy lived alone in a little two-bedroom wooden house at the back of the village. There were always colorful flags flying in front of her home. Heads of dolls were stuck on poles at the four corners of her plot. The scent of incense always filled the air around that area. She was always in bright red and white dresses and her head was always wrapped in black.

The villagers tried their best not to have any discourse with her. The only people who visited her were strangers from elsewhere in the country. Pompey, however, was always respectful and friendly towards her.

"Good morning, Mother Lucy," said Pompey.

"Hello darling, how yuh doing?" she inquired.

"So-so," replied Pompey.

Sensing something was amiss, she decided to pry into it. "Come, poopo, come and tell Mother Lucy wha' bothering yuh."

They sat together on a river stone, while water raced down the valley in the background. The bamboo trees creaked from friction against each other as the wind pushed on them. Birds sang sweetly in the mango tree over their heads. The scent of the river proved soothing to the nerves. Pompey took a deep breath and began relating his troubles to Mother Lucy. He spoke for an hour, even sobbing in between. Mother Lucy listened attentively, but never interrupted. Reaching across in between sobs, she would caress his shoulder and maintain eye contact. Her face reflected a pained expression, as if she shared in his grief.

At the end of his woeful tale, she pulled him to her bosom and comforted him in her warm, motherly embrace. "My child, Mother Lucy is going to help you, don't yuh worry your little head," she stated. "Come see Mother Lucy on Friday night as soon as the sun go down. Now, run along and cheer up. Leave everything to Mother Lucy, yuh hear?"

Pompey stood up, feeling lightheaded; his conscience felt clear and everything seemed brighter. Colors in the trees and vegetation seemed to amplify their vividness. He turned to the water and admired how it ran smoothly over the rocks, wishing that his life would imitate the water and rocks in his life. Taking another deep breath, he turned, exhaled, and headed home.

Friday evening, as soon as the sun blew its last kiss from the horizon, Pompey headed out to Mother Lucy's house. He took with him a flashlight to illuminate his path on the way back, for the road was rocky and he did not want a busted toe. As he got closer, he was greeted by frankincense riding the evening breeze. Every now and then, a bat would swoop by his head on its nightly excursion for food. The air was cool and fresh, as was normal for this area. No one was about, and that was good, for he did not want anyone nosing about in his business.

27

He entered the yard and knocked softly on the door. "Come in," came a cry from inside. Inside, he found himself standing in a neat little living room. In the middle was a small wooden table, covered with what appeared to be a blue cloth and a vase in the middle. The walls were unpainted and the ceiling was made of tin sheets. There were three chairs at a small dining room table and Mother Lucy was occupying one of them. Behind her on the wall stood an altar that had a bowl of fruit and two glasses of a clear liquid substance. In the center of the altar was an idol of a man with two axes and red and white bead necklace. He looked fierce.

"Come, sit down, darling," coaxed Mother Lucy, a huge smile covering her face. Pompey returned the smile and strode over to sit. "My child, I have been doing some thinking, and I believe the only way to help you is to give you a helper," stated Mother Lucy, staring into his eyes. "I am going to give you a child that you must birth.

"What, huh, how?" stammered Pompey.

"Relax, my child, relax," said Mother Lucy calmly. "Listen to what I have to say and follow my instruction without deviation and you will never know want. Don't follow them and you will wish you were dead!" exclaimed Mother Lucy ominously.

With that, she pulled out a black cloth that seemed to conceal an object. Placing the cloth on the table, she opened it to reveal a single large brown egg. Pompey's eye was drawn to it as if by a magnet. "I want you to place this egg under your left arm for 21 days. You can only remove it at night to bathe and sleep, but be sure to wrap it in this black cloth. Do not let anyone see it, or mention it. Twenty-one days from today will be the full moon. At midnight, go to the big silk cotton tree behind Gabby's house and do this.

"Standing straight with the egg under your arm, lift that arm up and quickly say, 'I am your master,' before the egg hits the ground. On hitting the ground, a little man will come out of the shell. If he comes out before you say, 'I am your master,' then he will rule over you and your life will be hell. If you're successful, you will be his master, and he will do all you ask. However, remember to feed him every full moon with milk and cake. Do not neglect to do so. If, when the time comes you wish to get rid of him, there is only one way. On the full moon, place the milk and cake in freshly cut and cleaned out calabash and as soon as he climbs in, cover it quickly with the black cloth that the egg was in. Then, go down to the sea and row out about a mile. Toss the calabash into the ocean and turn your back to it. Do not look back! On the way out, he will promise you the world or threaten you; his voice will appear as your mother, father, me, anyone you know, but do not speak to him or look back.

"Do you understand everything I have told you?"

"Yes, Mother Lucy, I will do all you instructed," replied Pompey nervously.

"Now take the egg and go," she stated. Pompey got up, took the egg in the black cloth, and left.

Pompey followed all the instruction to the "T," and at midnight on the 21st day, took up his position under the silk cotton tree. The moon was huge in the sky; one felt like you could reach out and touch it. There were a few scattered clouds here and there. The silk cotton tree's branches swayed back and forth to the rhythm of the breeze. Some parts of the tree shone silver; others black under the moonlight.

Pompey raised his arm and shouted, "I am your master!" The egg hit the ground and broke . . . *crack!* Out jumped a little creature! Pompey, even though he was told what to expect, was shaken, for he leaped back. His leg crashed into a log, sending him sprawling. The little creature ran up to where he had fallen. Turning to face the creature, he could not help but notice that it had grown to about a foot in height. He pulled himself to his feet and headed for home, the creature in tow.

At home in his room, he finally got a good look at the creature. It was black with green hair; its fingernails were long and black. Its eyes were green and its teeth yellow. The creature's body was quite muscular for a mini-look manlike being. Staring at Pompey, he said, "Master, what do you wish me do?"

Pompey replied greedily, "Make me the richest man in the village."

29

"As you wish," replied the creature, and it vanished into the air. Pompey could not sleep that night; he tossed and turned, looked under the bed all the time, but the creature was gone. He did not know when he fell asleep, but when he awoke, the sun was high in the sky. As his consciousness returned, he recalled his adventure last night and shot up straight. Looking all around the room and under the bed, behind the dresser, and in it also, there was no creature to be found. *All this was just a dream,* he thought, laughing, *what a dream!* Turning to the nightstand, he noticed a lottery ticket for the Windward Islands lottery for that night's drawing. Picking it up, he racked his brain. How in the world did that get there? And not for hell could he remember. Placing the ticket in a book, he went outside to use the outhouse.

Pompey was off that weekend from work and decided to paint the kitchen. He had promised his mother a month ago he would do so and, besides, he needed to borrow some money for a party later tonight. So he set to work. Two hours into it, his mother came home saying how lucky some people are. "What are you talking about, Ma?" he asked.

"Someone in St. Marks won three million dollars in the lottery," she said.

"Oh, I wish was me," he said jokingly. At the same moment, he remembered the ticket in the room and, dropping the paintbrush to the floor, sending paint everywhere, he ran into the bedroom for the ticket in the book. "Ma, what was the winning numbers?" he excitedly asked.

"Hold your horses; let me see where I put it," said Ma. "Mmmhm, yes, here it is," she exhaled.

Snatching the results from her hand, he compared them: 6-11-22-19-7-22, all lined up on his ticket. "Woii, ah win, ah win, ah win, woii," screamed Pompey.

"Let mi see da day boy," demanded Ma. "Woyo yo ,yo, yo, woii, yuh win, yuh win," bawled out Ma. They jumped up and down, and ended up kicking down the pan of paint. That only made them laugh all the more; they could buy a thousand more cans.

That is how the Blue Diamond was born. Things went smoothly, from then on. The creature appeared back on the full

30

moon, and Pompey fed it. Business blossomed at the Blue Diamond. People from all over Grenada came: some out of curiosity to see the lottery winner; some for a good party. Whatever their reason, they came. This went on for years. Pompey saw Mother Lucy twice after that; once after he won the money to give her fifty thousand, which she politely refused, and at her funeral five years later.

After seven years of feeding the creature, Pompey got fed up and besides, he had gotten all that he needed anyway. He decided that this coming full moon he was going to rid himself of this creature. So he got his calabash ready with the black cloth from the egg and bided his time.

The full moon came and Pompey placed the milk and cake into the calabash. The creature appeared and headed hungrily to the calabash to eat. As soon as he climbed in, Pompey corked the hole with the black cloth. A scream went up. "Ahha! Open up, you wicked ungrateful man, after all I did for you and your family," screamed the creature.

Pompey said nothing. He quickly picked up the calabash and headed for Crayfish bay. There he climbed in to the nearest boat and headed out. The night almost resembled the night he birthed the creature. The oars spliced the water, driving the boat forward. The creature pleaded that he would bring in twenty million this time, or any woman his heart desired would be his for the taking, if only he turned back. Pompey ignored the pleas, screams, or promises. About one mile out, he picked up the calabash and threw it into the ocean. He then turned his back to it and headed for shore.

There was silence, then halfway back he heard, "Pompey, my sweet child." Hearing Mother Lucy's voice, he turned around.

Later that night, the Blue Diamond caught fire and burned, leaving only the walls, Mr. and Mrs. Davis were cremated in the blaze. As for Pompey, he was never seen or heard from again. The villagers assumed the family all met a fiery end.

Today, there is a new tenant in Old Mother Lucy's house; he stands one foot tall and has beautiful green eyes.

Clyde Viechweg

The Black Mirror

Anne became the owner of Dry River estate in 1988. She had visited it years ago and had fallen in love with it at first sight. There are two ways to get there. From St. Georges, over the Grand Etang Mountains down to Birch Grove, make a right over the bridge that spans the great river.

Follow the hill all the way through St. James, passing a strong flowing spring next to the roadway, where the cool, refreshing water rejuvenates weary travelers.

Leaving there, we continue on, to the border of La Digue Village. At the border to the left lies the water works dams that provide water for surrounding villages. It is to this spot you would travel to if coming from Grenville, the second option for getting to Dry River.

Turn right onto the road next to the shop and follow the winding road through Bellevue land, passing the last of the houses. The pothole-filled road goes by Bellevue Estate and snakes its way through hills and lush vegetation, until a tiny, red mud pasture comes into view on the left.

At the back of the pasture, lie some small dams fed by springs deep into the mountains.

Driving on for thirty feet, we descend a little hill and over a concrete bridge, large enough to accommodate one vehicle at a time, and accelerate up a badly weathered road to the top. At the top, the road separates Brimington Estate on the right from Dry River Estate to the left.

Turning onto the gravel driveway next to a giant fir tree, a beautiful wooden plantation house stands majestically against a mountain backdrop. There are two round corners to the front of the house. A wall step leads up to a veranda that looks out on to Mount Saint Catherine into the distance. Enter its green door into the living room. The floor is constructed from green heartwoods and is stained to a black finish. The furniture consists of turn–of-the-century items. Green plantation shutters lie on each side of the doorway. From the living room, we walk into the dining room, where a large oak table stands in the center next to a window, looking up at the mountains. There are two doors on both sides of the head of the table that lead to the four bedrooms. Bypassing the living room, we enter into the kitchen that is the only concrete structure attached to the house.

It is comprised of a fireplace built for wood fire. There is a kerosene refrigerator bringing up the rear. There are cupboards and a small pantry too. There are no pipes with running water, nor is there electricity. The last of these luxuries terminated at the last house in Bellevue land.

Twenty feet from the back of the house is an old outhouse that sits on a slight incline.

Surrounding the house and fanning out are acres upon acres of fertile cultivated lands, covered in coffee, cinnamon, cloves, nutmeg, oranges, grapefruit, bananas, mangoes, and even a Chinese guava tree.

A huge cherry tree sits in the front yard under the right round corner of the house. There are no neighbors here, except for the occasional monkey troupe.

There sits a huge cast iron pot for catching runoff rainwater. The other source of clean drinking water comes from a spring to the back of the house on a hillside. There is another spring 300 meters west of the house.

All light at night is provided from lanterns, candles, and flashlights. It gets dark here early because of the cover of trees and vegetation.

So Anne settled into her secluded life with her sister as her companion. Anne had returned home after living and working in London for thirty-odd years. Her sister Joy was a widow with no children. Her husband died of mysterious complications two years ago.

Anne too was married, to a Nigerian man who was a doctor at the hospital from which she retired. He had decided that he would work for another year before retiring to join his wife.

Dr. Abu was a gifted surgeon who stood five feet nine inches tall. He had gained some weight in the last few years due to his busy and stressful schedule that resulted in poor eating habits.

34

His skin was of a healthy, smooth, ebony color complemented by a set of pearly white teeth. Dr. Abu was an intelligent chap who became a doctor at the age of twenty-three and a skillful surgeon at twenty-six. He was of a very quiet and reflective disposition. What no one knew outside of his family and wife was that he also a high priest of Ifa. Ifa is the religion of the Yoruba people of western Nigeria. As a high priest, he was skillful in preparing herbal medicine and invoking spiritual forces for divination purposes, or to bring about change in his or another person's environment.

Anne, every Friday, would drive into Grenville to pick up supplies and to speak to her husband on the phone from her friend Letty's house.

Glenda was Anne's sister, who was a frail-looking woman in her late fifties. She had snake- looking eyes that stared and seemed never to reflect light. She kept to herself and rarely left Dry River. For most of the month, she was less energetic in her movements. However, that changed around the full moon. Days before the full moon, she would become restless and energetic. Neither sister had any children or any other siblings. Both their parents had long passed on. Anne was a family-oriented person and she loved her sister.

It was around the full moon that Anne started getting sick. She woke up each morning of the three days the full moon lasted to black and blue marks on her arms and legs. Also, a nauseated feeling settled on her. All energy was drained from her body and she felt dizzy often. If she complained to her sister about her condition, Glenda would advise her to go to the hospital. Anne would go and have tests, run but nothing out of the ordinary was found. In fact, the doctor told her that she was healthy.

Anne's health would return after the full moon and the marks would disappear too. In her weekly phone conversations to her husband, she never mentioned the bizarre occurrences that took place around the full moon.

Two Fridays passed and Dr. Abu received no call from his wife. This was a cause for worry, for Anne was a very reliable woman. So he called Letty. Letty told him she had not seen her in two weeks; however, she had planned to go check on her the following day. She told him to call back around three o 'clock Grenadian time the next day for an update.

Letty arrived at Dry River Estate on Saturday morning. The place was mostly quiet, with the exception of the chuckling of a few chickens in between pecking for earthworms. Letty always liked visiting here for she found it so relaxing and refreshing. The wind made a pleasant sound as it made its way through the trees, invoking a peaceful spirit in Letty.

She made her way up the stairs to find the door slightly ajar. "Anneeee," she called out loud. "Where are you?" There came a muffled sound from the bedroom. "Anne, are you still in bed? Life in London, I see," she stated good-naturedly, followed by a chuckle.

"Letty, in here," came a weak response from the bedroom. Hearing the desperation in her friend's voice, Letty rushed into the bedroom to find her friend lying weakly on her bed.

"What is wrong with you? How long have you been like this? Where is your sister?" came a barrage of questions from Letty all at once.

"Glenda is on the land, picking up nutmegs," replied Anne. Anne then related to her best friend what happened to her once a month, pulling up her robe to reveal big, circular black and blue marks on her thighs.

"Oh my god," gasped Letty. "Come, I am taking you to the hospital," stated Letty firmly. Helping her friend to her feet, she supported her against her body and they made their way to Letty's car in the yard. She positioned her friend in the back seat of the car so she could lie down. She ran back into the house to leave a note for Glenda, letting her know that she was taking Anne to the hospital.

Letty rushed her friend to Mirabeau hospital. A doctor examined Anne in the emergency room and ordered the nurse to hook her up to an IV bag.

"Your friend is dehydrated and her blood pressure is very low. You did the right thing by bringing her here and thus saving her life. We will keep her here for observation over the next few days," said the doctor.

Letty spent the rest of the evening with her friend at the hospital. Looking out the window of the ward, she could not help but notice the stately palm trees that towered to the heavens. The trees and flowers gave the buildings a vibe more of a retreat center than of a hospital.

Letty told Anne that her husband was worried about her. "Didn't Glenda stop by and give you my message?" asked Anne.

"I have not seen your sister in three months," replied Letty.

"That's strange. I was too weak to go to La Bay last week, so she went instead. I told her to stop by you and to let you know of my condition and to let my husband know that I was under the weather and would call him when I felt better," said Anne, continuing, "when she got back home, she assured me that she had relayed my message to you."

"Probably she forgot; you know how that is," said Letty, trying to make light of the matter at the same time. "Anyway, I am saying 'good night' and will stop by in the morning to check on you, so get some rest," said Letty.

"Thank you so much, Letty," said Anne gratefully.

"You are so welcome, darling," replied Letty at the same time bending over to plant a kiss on her friend's cheek. With that, she left.

As Letty was walking into her house, she heard the phone ringing. She rushed in to answer. On the other end was Dr. Abu.

"Hello Letty, did you manage to go see my wife?" he asked desperately.

"Yes, I did," replied Letty. She then went on to relate the day's events to him. At the end, she reassured him all was well and that there was no need to worry, for Anne was expected to make a full recovery.

The doctor thanked her for being a true friend to his wife and expressed his gratitude to her. He told her that he had booked a ticket to Grenada that afternoon and that he would be there on Wednesday. They said their goodbyes.

Dr. Abu hung up the phone, but he could not shake the feeling that something supernatural was at work here. Tonight, he would consult the spirits.

At midnight, he went into his study. Moving back his desk, he took up a square piece of black board and hung it on the wall. He then lit three black candles and turned off the light. He stood facing the black board, perfectly still. Reciting an ancient incantation while concentrating all his energy to the center of the board, his physical eyes soon relaxed and he opened his third eye.

The black board soon got misty and as it cleared, he could make out his wife on the hospital bed, asleep. She looked so peaceful, it brought a joy to his heart, for he loved her deeply.

"Mirror, mirror whose eyes can see the future, past, or now. Show me what happened to Anne," chanted the doctor.

New images soon appeared; in them, he saw his sister-in-law Glenda standing in front of a huge silk cotton tree, naked on the full moon.

She was standing on one leg, looking at the moon. Bazil, the evil spirit that lived in the tree, was conversing with her, promising her more power in exchange for the blood of her sister.

He then entered her, transforming her into a Soucouyant and flying off to her sister's house. Entering through the keyhole in the sister's door, they began to drink greedily of Anne's blood. He could see Anne trying to wake up, but she was being held down and her eyes forced shut. Once they sated their thirst, they flew back to the tree and Bazil vanished into the tree trunk. Glenda pulled her skin back onto her body and found herself naked again. Putting her clothes on, she hurried home before the sun rose.

Dr. Abu knew that the world was full of evil, but even evil people love their own families. This was deep-seated evilness. He knew how much Anne loved her sister and that Glenda was all that was left of her kin. But he also knew that if he did nothing, his wife would soon die under mysterious conditions. In a rage, he commanded the mirror to show him Glenda. She was laying on her back, sound asleep. Seeing her comfortably in her bed at home while her sister lay in hospital due to her wickedness was too much for Abu to bear. Snatching a dagger, he plunged it into the center of the heart of the image of Glenda on the board. At that moment, Glenda sat up in bed, let out a blood-chilling cry, and collapsed back onto the bed dead.

The next morning, Letty went to bring breakfast to her friend Anne at the hospital. She found her friend back to her usual bubbly self. "Hello, Letty! Just in time. The doctor said I could go home today. I feel great too," said Anne, smiling from ear to ear. "Besides, I need Glenda to help me paint the living room too."

They drove to Dry River after Anne was discharged. Letty filled her in on her husband's phone call and that brought a smile to Anne's face. She could hardly wait to see him. At the house, they walked up the stairs.

"Glendaaaa," shouted Anne. There was no answer. "I am home, did you miss your sister?" inquired Anne jestingly. Hearing no reply, Anne went to check her sister's room. Glenda was lying on the bed. "You can't hear ah calling yuh?" asked Anne. No response. Anne sensed something was amiss and walked over to the bed and shook her sister. Glenda's body was stiff. "Oh god, nooo, noo!" cried out Anne loudly. Letty, who had gone to the kitchen for a glass of water, was startled by the crying and rushed to the room. There on the bed was Anne crying on top of her sister. Letty had no need to inquire; instead, she reached out and held her friend.

The funeral was five days later. There were few people who attended: Anne, Abu, Father David, Letty, and the funeral home workers to carry the coffin.

Abu held his wife as she sobbed, and kissed her forehead every so often. Letty noticed a sly smile on Dr. Abu's face when he looked at the coffin of Glenda. It invoked a sense of dread in her stomach for a split second, then it was gone.

Six months after the funeral, Dr. Abu retired and moved to join his wife Anne in Grenada. He shipped his personal effects too, among them a square piece of black board.

Clyde Viechweg

The Jacks that Blinked

WARNING: Before I begin to narrate this story, I must ask my female audience not to attempt any of the following alchemy in the tale. What goes around comes around. With the boundary of liabilities established, let us continue our tale.

Our character for this evening, I will call Roy, for the sake of concealing his identity. To sum up, Roy was not an easy equation, and if he were one, he would work out to be something like this: 1+1=3. You see, Roy was a customs officer by day and a Woodman* by night. Roy was a handsome fellow, who stood at six feet two inches tall. He had a most pronounced cheekbone that was indented by dimples, along with intelligent hazel eyes, and a straight nose and lips that always seemed to smile. He carried his head high with what might be mistaken for an air of superiority, but this was not the case, for Roy was down to earth.

At sports, he could hold his own with the best and his chiseled physique played a great part in that.

Whenever he played basketball after work, ladies always seemed to happen to walk by slowing down, with hopes of watching his chest heaving from exertion, while sweat ran down the contours of his chest into the furrows of his ripped abs and down again into what was not visible, but what the hell was the imagination for. All the subtlety was not lost on Roy, for he would always flash his milky smile in their direction, which never failed to bring blood rushing to their cheeks.

Every night, Roy was in some woman's bed in some different area of the island. His reputation soon was tarnished, helped along by jealousy and burnt conquests. Roy's mother pleaded with him every day to mend his promiscuous ways, but alas, it fell on deaf ears.

It finally was the tarnishing of his reputation that reduced his field of opportunity that made him decide to transfer to the customs office in Hillsborough, Carriacou, the sister isle north of Grenada.

Let us now sneak along for the move with Roy. Roy boards the *Osprey* ferry Sunday morning to make the twenty-something-mile trip that takes about an hour, depending on the sea and weather. It's a beautiful day; the skies are clear, there are cool breezes coming off the ocean and the seagulls riding the currents. As the *Osprey* pulls away from the dock, Roy breathes a sigh of nervous relief and settles down for the ride.

The *Osprey* makes its way out the harbor; it passes beneath Fort George and the General Hospital for the open channel. Roy looks on as the ferry glides over the serene water: at the new cruise ship terminal and mall, past the bus terminal and fish market. It's Sunday and it's quiet as usual, for the town is closed. He cannot help but notice the beauty and charm of the town in which he has lived all his life, but never paid much mind to. Viewing it from a different angle, he sees how it all came together: roads, hills, streets, houses, and business interlocking to form the organism called a town. A great sorrow swells up in his heart and he begins questioning his move. Hovering north over the fish market sits the colonial-built Catholic cathedral. To its left is St. Joseph's Convent in pink, and above that his alma mater Presentation Boys College in yellow. The National Stadium soon comes into view and stands proudly as a testament of change.

The Osprey engines are gunned and she takes off, splitting the water as God did the Red Sea. Cherry Hill, Fontenoy, Grand Mal, whip by quickly. Moliniere Point sits on a tip of land jutting out into the sea, which happens to be an underwater natural park that even has an art display of sculptures that form an artificial reef. Gouyave looms in the distance; yes, the town that never sleeps. At its sight, a great joy and pride settles in his heart, for it is here that Kirani James was born.

"Yes, sir, he put Grenada on the map when he brought home a gold medal from the 2012 Olympics in London," he reflects. Roy had jumped up and down in the street on the Lance to the music of Mr. Killa and had such a good time. He even strained his waist whining down to the ground with two women, but he did not mind for he had his medicine with him, a whole bottle of Woodman rum.

Soon they are outside of Sauterurs, Grenada's most northern town, with Carib Leap next to it. Carib Leap is where one of the two groups of original settlers to Grenada, the other being the Arrowak Indians, leapt to their death rather than be enslaved.

Grenada is soon in the distance and the waters start getting choppy. The *Osprey* is making its way through the infamous Kick-'em-Jenny or Mt. Kick-'em Jenny, which is an active submarine volcano that is known to make the water in the channel rough. Thankfully, today, she is not in one of her foul moods and Carriacou is soon seen in the distance. Pulling into the Hillsborough Bay, the *Osprey* meets azure blue tranquil water that lies submissively, welcoming you to her port.

Roy disembarks onto the jetty that runs into the heart of town. His friend and coworker is there to meet him. After exchanging pleasantries, they head to the guest area to check Roy in. If I could dare use the word idyllic and town in the same sentence, then I would have best described the capital of Hillsborough. The town exudes charm at every turn that lulls the visitor into a storybook setting.

Having checked in, Larry, Roy's coworker, takes him on a tour of the island. Carriacou is a tiny island that is 14 square miles. The population is, give or take, 7000 souls. The island is comprised of quaint and colorful villages like Belaire, Dumfries, Hermitage, and Top Hill. The main road runs through the island, but does not encircle it. A unique thing about the island is that the main road crosses the airstrip. So, whenever a plane is incoming or taking off, traffic is stopped from crossing the airfield.

The highest point on the island is in Dover and its mount stands at 955 feet. The view is breathtaking; the vistas of the rolling landscape dotted with Caribbean-style houses and color schemes that are enchanting. The blue sea seems to go on forever in all directions. Petit Martinique lies slightly northeast and the Grenadines and Tobago Keys falls behind it.

Now, let us return to our little drama.

43

Roy soon settled into his work and his old habits. In the three weeks since his arrival, he had broken nine hearts. However, one of them decided that she was going to be that man's wife if it was the last thing she ever did. Enter Gertrude.

Gertrude was a quiet and simple girl, who lived with her grandma in the village of Belaire. Her parents lived in Canada with her other siblings. She came on holiday one year and never left. She was the apple of her grandma's eye and they seemed to do everything together. There were whispers though in the village that Gertrude's grandma was an Obeah woman. Gertrude did not care what anyone said about her sweet granny, for Grandma was a loving, wise, and thoughtful woman. She had an uncanny way of predicting events and of lives of the village people, which Gertrude reasoned was due to Grandma's intelligence.

As it happened, Grandma noticed Gertrude's sadness and sensed that her heavy heart was burdened by sorrow and despair. Subtly inquiring from Gertrude what was the matter, it all came out in a flood of sobs. She had hidden her relationship with Roy from Grandma, and for this, she was sorry. He had asked her not to disclose their relationship yet to her grandma until he could propose to her. This she now realized was never his intention. However, she loved him with all her heart and she could not envision life without him. She cried and cried, while Grandma held her in her arms. Had Gertrude looked up, she would have seen the fire in Grandma's eyes and the evil grin spread over her face, but Grandma's embrace was too comfortable to leave. She drifted off to sleep.

When she got up, she felt somewhat refreshed. Turning while she stretched, she noticed Grandma sitting in a chair by the bed. "Hi, Grandma," she greeted her.

"How much do you really love this man?" Grandma asked.

"I would die for him!" replied Gertrude strongly.

Grandma stared at her for a moment, like someone who was about to make the biggest decision of their life. "My child, I am going to help you get your man back, however once we go this route, there is no turning back." Gertrude jumped out of bed and hugged Grandma so tightly, she gasped.

"Really, really, Grandma?!" she shouted in joy.

"Come now, put on your shoes and come outside and help me bring something inside," said Grandma.

They stepped out into the cool evening. The sun had just sunk on the horizon and twilight was making its appearance. She followed Grandma to the back of the house to the little garden shed. The shed was in disrepair, with grass and vines all over it. The windows were broken and a single rusted wagon wheel rested against the side. Grandma put on her flashlight and opened the door. It creaked eerily on its hinges. Inside the dimly lit room, the smell of musty dry rotting wood was prevalent. "There is what I am looking for!" cried Grandma, pointing to an old wooden chair in the corner. They pulled it out and dragged it back inside the house. The chair was made of mahogany wood and was varnished to a black finish. It was the size of a rocking chair, with an armrest and a high back. There appeared to be some stylized sigils markings on the seat. Grandma dusted the chair and commenced to clean it with soap and water. When she was done, it stood beautifully complementing the living room.

"Grandma, why did you leave this beautiful chair outside for so long?" asked Gertrude.

"This chair is an enchanted chair that my mother gave to me. It's the chair that kept my husband at home all his life," whispered Grandma. "Whoever sits in it feels a compelling need to not leave the house, for Papa Lebo guards it. This is the first half of returning your love to you. The other part you must do on your own, following my instructions carefully. The chair can only keep them at home, but to steal their heart requires other measures. When next is your period?" asked Grandma.

"It started this morning," replied Gertrude.

"The spirits favor you, my child," said Grandma. "Listen well, for this is the part that is to steal his heart for you. Tomorrow morning, run down to Jew Bay. The fishermen will be pulling their nets. Grab the two big jacks if you can or any other size will do. Do this before anyone touches them. Do not speak to anyone on the way or back. Wrap the jacks in newspaper so that the sunlight does not shine upon them, for that could cause our plot to fail because the sun chases evil away," warned

45

Grandma. "At home, put on a pot of rice and peas to cook and fry up the jacks nice and dry. When the rice cooks, put place the jacks onto the rice. Place the pot on the floor and stoop over the pot, letting the steam come up between your thighs and recite the following incantation: *'A string ah tie, A knot ah make, his heart ah take, come papa Lebo and put Roy in he place!'* Nine times this should be recited, while tying a knot at the end of each incantation, so at the end there should be nine knots. Take that string and put it in the pot of rice and stir it nine times in an anti-clockwise direction, the reason being is that we are working against in nature. Take this food to him and in nine days he will be yours forever," ended Grandma's instruction.

Gertrude got up early the next morning and did all she was told. At noon, she was in front of the customs in Hillsborough with Roy's lunch. Roy was not pleased to see her, for he was dating a new chick. However, he was hungry and the scent of the food made his mouth water. "Thanks for the lunch, but I have a girl friend," he said, eyeing the basket hungrily.

"That's okay. I have moved on myself and as a token of friendship, I brought you this," stated Gertrude with jealousy pangs in her stomach upon hearing about his new love. Turning quickly, she left before he could see the jealousy in her eyes.

Roy quickly ate the lunch and admitted to himself that was the best food he had ever had. He found himself daydreaming an hour later about how good it would be to come home to a lunch like this every day. Gertrude even looked better since the last time he saw her too. *Maybe I had made a mistake in ending that relationship so quickly,* he thought. Strangely, for the rest of the week, he thought only about Gertrude; how pretty her smile was, her laughter, the light in her eyes, the sweetness of her embrace, and the grace her hips swung with as she walked. In his conversations, he would reference things to her. Of course, his new love tired of it and left. This brought a relief to his spirit. Sure enough, as wise, old Grandma had foretold, nine days later, Roy found himself at the door of Gertrude. Gertrude was delighted as he wooed her with sweet words of his undying love for her and told her how her beauty could only be surpassed by the ocean and not by any woman dead or alive. Grandma came out the house and invited him in. Seeing him, she realized how easy it was for her granddaughter to fall in love with him. She was 75 years old and in all her life, she had never laid eyes on such a fine specimen as now stood in front of her. "Please come in and have a seat," she offered. Roy walked inside and he was directed to the old mahogany chair by the window. The chair looked so inviting and he quickly took a seat.

Should I bother to continue with this tale? Okay, if you insist.

Roy and Gertrude were inseparable from that day. They got married and had two beautiful kids. Roy rushed home everyday to be with his family. All who knew him could only shake their heads in wonder at his transformation.

Grandma has since passed. However, if you're ever in Carriacou and happen through the village of Belaire, look for the blue and white wooden house on the hill next to the Tamarind tree, and you will be sure to see Woodman Roy in his chair by the window, looking out on Jew Bay.

*Woodman- Promiscuous man

Clyde Viechweg

The Son of Shango

The son of Shango sat erect across from the bonfire. He was half-naked; his ebony skin seemed to glow from the reflected light of the fire. The night was very cool, but it mattered not, for he basked in the warmth of the flame.

On the other side of the fire, three drummers beat tirelessly on the goatskin cover that stretched tightly over the hollow wooden frame that formed the drums. Sweating profusely, their hands rose and fell in sync with each other, producing a hypnotic frequency that stirred the latent forces in all the souls around the fire.

Shango's son stared fixedly into the fire, his body perfectly still. Embers crackled under the intense heat, while others leapt from the flame.

In his body, the hypnotic beat of the drums pulled back the veil that obscured the physical world from the spiritual. In the flames, he saw his father dancing, calling to him to come join.

"Come my son; come rest, your work is done," a voice seemed to call from the flame.

Closing his eyes, he reflected on the journey that started many, many moons ago in another land.

Before he became the son of Shango, he was once someone else's child. The land he ended up being born on had changed its name four times: Camahogne by the Carib Indians, Conception Island by Columbus, la Grenade by the French, and finally, Grenada today

He was born to Pierre and Maire Fedon. His father had been a landholder on the island of Martinique and his mother a house slave from Haiti, brought to Martinique and sold to his father's estate.

His mother and father fell in love. Pierre's father was not pleased, so the couple moved south to La Grenade and they got married in 1759.

In 1763, Juilen Fedon was born to them at St. Marks. Two years later, they would move to the Belvedere Estate, in the parish of St. Johns. The estate was vast, with its lands stretching all the way into the other parish of St. Andrews.

There were fifty slaves that worked the field and ten that tended the house. Pierre Fedon demanded a hard day's work from them; however, he gave them the weekend off. The slaves then used this opportunity to hunt, plant their personal crops, and to worship their deities.

So it was into this atmosphere that young Julien Fedon grew up in. His father taught him how to read and write, bookkeeping, estate management, and to shoot. However, it was to be his mother that was to impact his life like no other.

Maire's mother was of the Yoruba tribe and she had been taken from her homeland in Dahomey, West Africa and was sold into slavery on the Caribbean island of Saint Domingue.

On the island, she gave birth to Maire alone, for Maire's father had escaped into the hills and he was never seen again while she was pregnant.

Maire grew up on the island of Saint Domingue until she was seventeen. In those years, she embraced Vodou and rose to become a Mambo (priestess). Yes, Ogun, the spirit of war had chosen her for his daughter.

Ogun blessed her and guided her, taking her to Martinique and unto Grenada to marry into a rich family. Maire loved Ogun, her deity, and kept an altar to him. It was she who led the slaves at Belvidere Estate in service on weekends. She became highly respected and feared.

As Juilen Fedon grew up, she began to educate him on his African heritage and in Vodou.

Maire explained to her son, that Vodou was a combination of many elements from other African tribes: the Bakongo people, the Yourba, the Taino Indians on Saint Domingue, as well as Roman Catholicism and mysticism.

He was taught that Vodouists are servants of the spirits and that Bondye' was the unknowable and unapproachable creator god, who never interfered with human affairs.

Instead, their prayers were directed at all times to the Ioa, who was the offspring of Bondye'.

Fedon learned that each Ioa directed certain aspects in his life. They revealed all the possibilities of life that they presided over. Through their mysterious powers, they controlled the world and the affairs of men.

The Ioa were to be honored through offerings, song, music, and dance, so that they may descend and take possession of someone and thus reveal spiritual truths to all.

Maire told him of Papa Legba, the guardian of the crossroads, the Marasa, Bondye' first children, and then there was Erzuile Freda, the spirit of love. Simbi was the spirit of the magicians and rain, while Kouzin Zaka was the spirit of agriculture.

Fedon absorbed everything his mother taught him and the spirits favored him in all he did. She showed him how to perform a variety of sorcery, to use a wide array of poisons, and even how to create the feared Zombie by using parts of the puffer fish mixed with other secret herbs.

When the day of his sixteenth birthday came — the day one of the Ioa would take him for their son — this day was his initiation.

All day long, food was cooked. There were rice and peas, yams, potatoes, calliou, breadfruit, goat, fish, and chicken. As soon as the sun went down, the estate yard was packed with devotees of the Ioa.

Service began with prayers, soon followed by songs and drums. Then Hounto, the spirit of the drums, was honored. With the building crescendo of the drums, songs for all the Ioa were sung, starting with the Legba family, and then into songs to the Gede family of spirits.

It was around midnight, while dancing and singing, lost in the enchanting enfoldment of the proceedings that Fedon looked in the fire and saw him: Shango, the god of fire, lightning, and thunder. He was smiling at him. Fedon felt energy racing around his body and a fire raging in his center. Suddenly, out of nowhere came a flash of lightning straight into the fire, sending embers flying. The drumming stopped suddenly, along with everyone. Only Fedon seemed not aware of what had transpired,

51

for he was standing in a circle of fire caused by the lightning strike.

All who saw shook with fear, for they knew that the person standing in that circle now was the son of Shango. His father had even reached out of heaven for all to see his blessings on his child.

Fedon collapsed to the ground and he saw a vision. A six-headed monster rose up out of the sea. He went into battle against it. He wounded the first head badly, but he was attacked by the second head, which he could not withstand, for he was weak from the first fight. So he fled to a faraway land. The monster followed, determined to slay him. The third, fourth, and fifth heads he slew, but in the end, the sixth found him at his most vulnerable and he was slain, falling on his own sword.

When he awoke, he was in his room and the sun was high in the sky. His mother was sitting next to his bed, smiling at him. There was a proud look on her face, yet a sadness in her eyes; her face was a contradiction of emotions. Maire knew that Shango having come with such force could only mean one thing: that Fedon was chosen for a huge task and great responsibility. She knew that could never be accomplished without heavy sacrifice, maybe even the loss of her son's life.

Over the next five years, she taught him everything to prepare him for the stormy road ahead. Fedon learned from his mother that the ritual of Shango was to develop self-control and thus mastery over himself. He was given the Shango beads that balance the yin and yang energies.

When he turned twenty-one, his father and mother deeded the estate to him and returned to Martinque to take over Pierre's father's estate, for he had passed away.

A year ago, the island was restored to Britain under the Treaty of Versailles. Young Fedon cared not for the British, for he found them arrogant and warlike. Besides, since he was of a mixed stock, he was not respected. Also, being a huge landowner on a small island brought jealousy. He found the conditions under which the slaves were working for the British very distasteful. The truth be told, he knew it was only a matter of time before he might lose everything.

Under the French, his family had strived and conditions were better. Around this time, he befriended Joachin Philip. He was a mulatto and worried about his fate too under British rule. The two of them grew up loving French classical history.

Fedon's historical idol was King Louis XIV of France. He loved that the king chose the most powerful of all physical things as his emblem, the sun. The sun was also associated with Apollo, god of peace and of the arts. The sun spread its rays evenly on all peoples no matter what their race or creed. The king enjoyed one of the longest reigns in European history.

He noted that King Louis kept all his nobles close to him so he could keep an eye on them. He played them one against the other for his attention. They were always guessing his next move, for he kept none in his confidence.

Fedon dreamed of being a great king like Louis. Little did he know, to be careful what you wish for.

In 1789, with the breakout of the French Civil War, a great desire arose in him to rid Grenada of British colonial rule, at the same time destroying the great evil of chattel slavery.

To this end, he had company, his best friend Joachin Philip. They formed a council of three landowners and started laying a plan for a revolt. Using his Houngan status among the slaves, he recruited other Houngans and Bokors on other plantations for the cause.

On the night of March 2nd, 1795, leading a force of 110 slaves and coloreds, he swooped down onto the town of Grenville, killing a large number of white English settlers. In another coordinated attack, his best friend made a swift and successful attack on Charlottetown.

For over a year, Fedon was the virtual ruler of ninety percent of Grenada.

With the arrival of German mercenaries, together with slave soldiers and British regiment troops forming a force of fifteen thousand, Fedon was forced to retreat in his mountain stronghold on his estate called Morne Vauclain and today Fedon's Camp.

It was here on this mountain that his father, Shango, visited him in a dream again. "My son, you have slain the first of the six-headed beasts, the second is coming. You cannot win, for I have other plans for you. In two days, a ship will leave for Saint Domingue, the birthplace of your mother. Disguise yourself and seek passage. I will clear your path of obstacles. There the other Houngans are waiting for you; there are five and they seek a sixth head for great work I have prepared you for. Now rest, my son," spoke Shango.

Two days later, Julien Fedon left Grenada on a ship to Saint Domingue, telling no one, for his father Shango wanted it that way.

Arriving in Saint Domingue, he was met by an old Bokor priest who saw him coming in a pail of water the day before. The spirit compelled him to the pier. Seeing Fedon disembark, he walked up to him and greeted him. They exchanged their secret handshake and word only the highest-ranking Houngans and Bokor would know.

They hurried off the pier before anyone might recognize Fedon. "You need a new name," said the old man.

Fedon thought for a moment before replying, "I have thought about one on my trip over here." The old man never bothered to ask what.

They arrived later at a village high in the mountains where they were met by four other men. Among the four, two were to become known to the world as Toussaint Louverture and Jean Dessalines.

"My brother," the four men shouted as they greeted Fedon.

"We have heard about your fierce fighting and strong leadership of our brothers in Grenada," stated Toussaint. "We hope you will bless us with that spirit here," he continued.

"It's time," interrupted the old man. They all turned quietly to face him. The old Bokor walked over to the fence, untied a big white goat, and began walking towards the mountain path. They all followed quietly.

They walked for nearly a mile through dense vegetation, over scattered rocks, and hills. At the top of the hill, they stopped in front of a large boulder, which had strange markings. The old man instructed them to light a fire in the middle of the small plateau.

54

Having done this, they circled the goat and began chanting invocations. This they kept up for three hours. When enough energy was in the circle, the old man ran the edge of the sharp dagger across the neck of the goat. Warm blood spilled onto his hands. They all cupped their hands and drank deeply. With their bloody hands, they drew sigils across their foreheads. The old man in the meantime had poured blood in the crevice of the rock.

The rock soon began to emit a green glow and started vibrating. The old Bokor then began reciting an old primordial incantation in an unknown language that none of them knew. At that moment, a giant bolt of lightning struck the giant rock, splitting it into two. In the middle emerged a huge red and black snake with a diamond in the center of its head. Fire blazed where its eyes were supposed to be. The snake then slithered over to the six priests. The old Bokor then took the dagger and cut his finger and everyone else's in the circle. The snake licked the blood hungrily. It opened its mouth wide and three little silver snakes pitched out. One went into Toussaint, one into Dessalines, and the other into Fedon. The snakes entered their stomachs with energy so powerful that it knocked them out. The huge snake then blew a mist over the men, thus blessing their venture and looking forward to feasting on the blood, which would be spilled on the battlefield.

The snake then faded into the darkness.

The old Bokor, with the help of the other two, revived the other three. They then made their way quietly down the mountain.

From that day onward, they battled and drove the French colonial powers out of Haiti. Fedon became a lieutenant under Toussaint and distinguished himself in battle. The mighty spirits moved in their souls, igniting them with an obsession towards freedom.

He had even defeated the three other heads of the great beast: the French, the British, and the Spanish invasion. There stood only one left.

So, here he was after all these years sitting in front of a bonfire on a very cool evening in Milot, Haiti, with the drums pounding and his father dancing in the flame coaxing him to come home. "Yes, Father, soon," he promised.

Looking back, he noted his childhood dream of being king had come through. However, he had not united the entire country of Haiti. He had ruled like his idol Louis XIV, as a despot. He had distributed plantations to his generals and brought prosperity to him subjects. From 1811 to today, 1820, he was king.

However, a week ago, the sixth head struck with lightning speed, like he had done in Grenville many moons ago. It struck in the form of a paralytic stroke. Now, all his enemies sensed his weakness and they were closing in. Revolts erupted everywhere and this time he could not quell them. Yes, his father Shango had shown him this day would come when he was sixteen years old, during his initiation, and, yes, Father Shango was always right.

The drums had stopped beating now; a serene silence carpeted the night. Turning in pain, he picked up the revolver on the table and cocked it. *Before I go, I must tell you my other name. I am Julien Fedon of Belvidere estate St. John, Grenada. I came to Haiti and became Henry Christophe, or as I have been called for the last nine years, King Henry I of Haiti.*

Turning to face his waiting father in the flames, he put the pistol to his head and fired.

Note from the author: I received this story in a dream, by an entity claiming to be Julien Fedon.
However, after some research, I found there is no record of the early life of Fedon or Christophe. In fact, the disappearance of Fedon brings on the arrival of Christophe. Here, historians can only speculate on Christophe's early life. So I invite you, the reader, to research the history of these men or man and to form your own conclusions.

The Lady in the Black Dress

If you take the scenic route along the western main road from the capital of St. Georges, you will find yourself bombarded by landscapes of green vegetation and multicolored homes to your right, while your senses would amplify at the azure waters of the Caribbean Sea to your left. If you're not busy, why not stop and have a drink and some food at the Iguana Bar in Fontenoy? Continuing north, you will pass through the quaint villages of Grand Mal, Molinere, Happy Hill, and come finally to the setting of this story.

Beausejour bay and Brizan are idyllic villages set a stone's throw from the ocean. The main road runs through, reducing whatever little flat land there is. There are a few scattered houses under the roadway, while others take the high ground above the road. Expansion is checked by the sharp rise of a rocky mount above the road and by the ocean at the bottom.

The people who live here are a close knit society; everyone knows everyone's business, or so they used to think up until three months ago, when the tranquility of their village was broken by what the newspaper dubbed, "psychic phenomena." When the storm passed, two of their own were dead, countless others traumatized.

Three months ago, two idle brothers were going through an old box of their deceased grandfather's personal effects in search of valuables, when they came across a copy of an old black magic manual. This brought their search to a standstill. They had heard rumors that their grandfather had made a deal with the devil for money in exchange for his soul. Grandpa had three fishing boats, two shops, and two buses when he was alive. These were now in their father's possession.

Dave and James loved money with a passion, but they loved spending it even more. The problem was they never seem to have any, because whatever little was given to them was squandered on strong drink and women. Having told you what they loved, I will tell you what they hated most: work! Their father pleaded with them to help run the shops or buses, but they always dodged him. So, a month ago, he cut off their allowance to pressure them into working. It was under this pressure that had brought them together that morning. rummaging through Grandpa's things in search of something of value to sell. Finding the book, they realized that there might be some truth to the rumors they had heard about Grandpa. They were too selfish to worry about Grandpa's reputation. What interested them was how they were going to use it to get rich.

Pushing the trunk back under the bed, they took the dusty book to their room and locked the door. The book had a black, worn out leather cover that gave it an ancient look. The book was held shut by a leather string that attached to two metal clips. Unbinding it, they discovered that it was written in old English text. In the table of contents, they found chapters on many spells. The one that caught their attention most was the "Money Slave" spell. Turning the page to it, they found a warning that said, "Don't turn the page unless you're willing to forfeit your soul."

"Man, hurry up and turn the damn page," commanded Dave, at the same time reaching over James to do so.

"Take it easy, man. I don't want to go to hell," replied James in a concerned tone.

"Hell? Hell is right here; we broke and that causes us enough pain and suffering," snapped Dave.

"Well, I was just saying..." James started replying.

"Hush yuh coward arse and gimme the book if yuh 'fraid," said Dave forcefully.

Grabbing the dusty book from James, he turned the page. On the page, there were drawings of a grave with six candles set on top of it. A coffin was open and a skeleton sitting upright. A figure in a black hooded robe with a red cord tied around its waist and a book open in its hands made up the rest of the illustrations.

They spent the rest of the afternoon reading and going over the spell until they felt it was their second nature. Then, all that was left to do was wait. You see, the spell could only work with the new and waxing moon. To complete the formula, they would need a white fowl cock, six black candles, a knife, and two pounds of salt.

The new moon came two weeks later and the brothers were excited. For those last two weeks, they discussed about how they would spend the money. They would each buy a sports car, take trips to Trinidad to spend some time at the brothel, and they would wear new suits of clothes every day. Yes, they had big plans. If only things would go as we wish. Huh mmmh!

Two weeks earlier, they had found an old grave next to a tree in the mangrove 100 meters from where the river met the sea. It was isolated and if anyone was passing on the main road and saw the candle light, they would assume it was someone crabbing. Reaching the grave, they placed the six candles in the shape of a cross on the grave and lit them. Dave then poured the salt around the grave to form a circle. James, meanwhile, was trembling in fear. However, he dared not back down in fear of his twin brother's temper. Taking the pillowcase, he pulled the cock from it. The cock scratched and kicked, then it crowed as loudly as if to send a farewell message with the night. Dave pulled the blade of the knife over its neck, sending the warm blood flowing over his hands and onto the grave. The night became electrified, as lightning flashed three times on the horizon. Poor James' knees were buckling. Dave then stood at the foot of the grave and recited the following: "*As above, so below, oh mighty keeper and guardian of the door;*

Give to us a helper, to make our path smooth; quicken the one who rest here beneath the moss; allow us to be his boss; and in return our soul will be lost!"

Dave had to this say thirteen times. On the 13th time, the ground started shaking with a great force and the mound in the grave started growing outwards, until it broke open to reveal what was once an old rotted pine casket. James was holding on to Dave so tightly that no breeze could pass between them. They stood speechlessly, looking into the hole, but there was not even a skeleton in the rotted box. Then all of a sudden, they both felt a pair of cold, clammy hands on their shoulders. They spun around in terror, coming face to face with a lady in a black dress.

"Why have you disturbed my rest, why, why!" she screamed.

59

This proved too much for poor James." "Oh God, yuh-yuh-yuh hear wha-what she say, Dave?" stammered James. "Woii ah go deaden right here," cried James.

"Ah sorry miss . . . ah sorry for waking yuh, go back and rest eh," said Dave, trembling...

"Yes, go back and sleep, the night still young," cried James with his hands over his face. *Wap, wap!* was the sound of two hard slaps that landed across James' cheeks from the woman.

"You too damn stupid," stated the woman coldly.

With that, they took off running, through the mangrove to the main road and homeward. They heard a blood curdling scream coming from the swamp. At home, they put on all the lights and hid in the bathroom. Ten minutes later, they could hear a woman's high heel shoes stomping up and down the road. A voice followed the shoes. "Why have you disturbed me? Come, come outside. I have something for you." This was kept up for 15 minutes. Dogs started barking and lights started coming on. Then it stopped!

Daylight came and Dave and James felt relieved. They ventured outside to hear neighbors talking about a crazy woman who was screaming last night. But no one had any idea of who it was.

For the next week, the village was quiet until that Sunday evening. Around 9 p.m., a group of four guys was lyming (hanging out) on the side of the road, when out of nowhere a lady in a black dress and high heel shoes suddenly appeared. This startled them. She peered into each one of their eyes and then vanished. They took off, screaming, "Help, woii, spirit, help!"

Neighbors came running out to see what was causing all the commotion. The boys breathlessly related what had transpired. Some told them to stop smoking weed; others, that what they thought they saw, they did not, while a few believed them. Of all the villagers who came outside to see the ruckus, two dared not show their face. Yes, we are talking about Dave and James. At that moment, they were trembling under the sheets.

"Yuh think she go find us?" asked James.

"No, she don't know where we live," replied Dave.

60

"We did not finish the spell; she won't stop until she find us.... Oh God... What did we do?" cried James. Dave just pulled the covers tightly, but remained silent.

Over the next month, the lady in the black dress would be seen by many more people. She even walked into a rum shop, kicked down a table of drinks, and then vanished. Others said they saw her whining down at a blocko. The rumors swirled around the village, then the parish, and finally the whole island knew. People made trips from around the island to catch a glimpse of this woman, but she never appeared. The villagers, however, dared not leave their homes after seven at night.

One evening after 8 p.m., Mr. Roy was making his way home when he bumped into the lady in the black dress. "I beg you pardon, miss," he apologized quickly. Looking at her, he could not see her face in the darkness. "What are you doing out here so late anyway? Yuh did not hear ah spirit on the loose," Roy joked.

"Oh no, I don't believe in such nonsense," replied the lady sweetly. And in the same breath, she asked, "What about you? You ain't fraid spirit?"

"Me fraid spirit, ha ha, spirit could kiss me arse. I have been on Earth now for 80 plus years and the only spirit I know is River Antonie rum," said Roy and then burst out laughing. The lady in the black dress stood quietly with a wicked smile on her face. "By the way, who is yuh?" asked Roy.

"An old friend, Roy," she answered.

"Well, wait nah, yuh know old Roy?" he asked. Roy shifted his body to get a better look at the lady. All of a sudden, a feeling of familiarity arose in him, yet this could not be, for that person had died when he was just a boy. However, come to think about it, her voice sounded the same but that could not be, for she was dead now for 70 years, thought Roy. "Yuh remind me of ah lady ah use to know when ah was just a little boy; her name was Miss Janet. She, however, passed," said Roy.

"Oh, too bad, I would have loved to meet her," replied the lady.

"Meet her; the only way yuh would have meet her was if yuh went by her to practice Obeah," stated Roy. "Who di arse making joke wid she."

"Well I see yuh did not care much for her," stated the lady.

"Well she was meh cousin and meh family kept us away from her. As for meh, I don't believe in that shit. When she dead, they bury the poor woman in the Mangrove, away from everything. People too fricking coward; look around, everybody inside because they 'fraid some spirit. Me, ah just drink meh rum and ah heading home; the spirit can kiss me arse," Roy boldly stated.

"Yuh is something else wii," laughed the woman. "By the way, I am looking for my two cousins, Dave and James. Yuh know where they live?"

"Yuh related to them two nastiness!" exclaimed Roy. "Them is two blight, deh does harass meh when ah drink meh rum, but ah tell them, one of these days ah go floor dem," Roy angrily stated.

Putting her hand on Roy's shoulder, she said, "Come, doh work up your nerves over dem, they always disturbing people rest. After tonight, yuh won't have a problem with them ever again," said the lady.

"Well how yuh hand so cold? Yuh doh have blood in yuh body?" joked Roy.

"Them nastiness live right there," Roy said while pointing out the house. They walked together towards the house. "They sleeping, I ain't see no light on," said Roy.

"That's good, ah doh like lights," said the lady. "Well, thank you for walking me here; I will see yuh in fifteen years," said the lady in black.

"In fifteen years? Old Roy will long be gone," said Roy.

"No, Roy, I have a strong feeling that you will be around," said the lady with a sly smile on her face.

"All right, darling, yuh too sweet. If yuh was ah little older, ah would have married yuh," flirted Roy.

"Yuh too young for meh, Roy," said the woman. They both gave a little laugh and parted ways.

James and Dave were sound asleep. They felt something cold on their feet, at the same time as the covers were being pulled from their bodies. They both opened their eyes and turned to the foot of the bed. Standing there was the lady in black. They tried to scream, but no sound came out, nor could they move. The lady moved towards them, her face distorted, her eyes glowing, and the evilest of grins on her face.

The next day, Dave and James were found dead. They were found with their eyes and mouths wide open, and a look of terror frozen upon their faces.

The woman was never seen again. However, Mr. Roy every so often reminisces about his encounter with the charming lady in the black dress.

Phantom Pregnancy

Marva was what some would call beautiful; to others she was stunning, and to me, she was my world.

Looking back on it, I can honestly say she was my first love. I first laid eyes on her back in '91 at intercollegiate track and field games. It was held at the Queen's Park pavilion back in those days. I can still hear the shouts, cheers, and songs echoing in my ears. "SAAS is the hardest; we come from the country and mash up everybody." PBC boys and their fans bellowed back, "PBC, we want it; we want ah gold." This went on all over the arena.

BBQ smoke filled the air, along with the vibrations of drums and other innovative musical instruments. There were snow cones, honey-roasted peanuts, and high spirits everywhere.

It was under this festive atmosphere that our paths crossed at the snow cone cart. She was dressed in her St. Joseph Convent uniform: pleated dark blue skirt, white starched shirt, and blue and white striped tie. Her hair was pulled back into one braid, which exposed her eyes to more sunlight, creating little sparkles, along with a mischievous smile that all proved too intoxicating for me.

I don't know where I found the courage to approach her, but I did. "Excuse me, princess, may I have a word with you?" I rambled.

Turning to me, she flashed a smile that revealed a set of pearly white teeth. "Yes, you can," she gaily replied.

"Do you go to Covent?" I stupidly asked.

"Ah, Ray Charles could see that!" she teasingly replied, sensing my nervousness. I could have kicked myself for being foolish. "Come, walk with me," she said, at the same time touching my arm, as to point the direction she wished to go. This sent quivers through me and my heart skipped a beat or two. Turning without a word, I followed her.

We walked outside to a big tree next to the river and talked and talked, while time passed as if it was one of the sprint

65

events. She told me about her family, the music she liked, the food she loved, what she wanted to become in the future. I listened attentively, for her every word was like music to my ear.

"Marva, there you are. I have been looking all over for you!" exclaimed a voice, thus breaking the spell I was under.

"Hi, Roxanne, this is Sancho. Sancho, Roxanne," Marva introduced us. We made some small talk until it was time to leave. I walked them to their bus. It was a blue Nissan and its name was, "Same damn ting." This bus would take her to Happy Hill where she resided. She wrote her number on a piece of paper and handed it to me as she boarded the bus.

From that time on, we became inseparable. We both graduated a few months later. That summer we went to the beach every other day, to the waterfalls, and to the movies. I grew to love her more with each passing day and could not imagine life without my sweetheart. I remember our first kiss too; it was soft, sweet, and lasted for an eternity. My eyes were closed, but I swear I saw every star in the heavens.

In September, the CXC results came out and our fate was cast. Marva got nine subjects with nine distinctions, making her the island scholar. I got six with three distinctions and three twos. We decided to work for two years, then go away to school. So we sent out applications and waited.

Marva was hired a week later at Barclays Bank and I was hired a month later at Scotia Bank. It was over our celebration dinner one Friday that Marva told me her friendship with Roxanne was over. When I inquired as to why, she told me that Roxanne was jealous of her, for doing well in exams and getting a job and all the attention she was receiving. Also, since she started seeing me, they hardly spent any time together. She said she had tried reaching out to her friend, but Roxanne told her she hated her, who the hell did she think she was, how ungrateful she was; that she had, had a crush on me a long time now.

Marva said she had asked her why she did not say anything before about her feelings for me. She had replied that she knew that she was not my type. They had screamed at each other and then stomped off in different directions, vowing never to speak to each other ever.

How was I to know that event was to change our lives forever? How could I ever imagine youth could fester such evil inclinations? That jealousy knew no bounds? How, tell me, how was I to know?

Marva and I started having sex later that year and could not seem to get enough. So it came as no shock when one day she announced to me that she had missed her period for three months now. A child was not in our plans. However, we decided to let our parents know. Marva's mother started crying, saying she was throwing away her future. Her dad was angry at me too. What had hurt Marva most was in his disappointment he had reserved for her. My parents took it lighter, I reckon, because I was a boy and boys do crazy and wild things. Three months later, all was forgiven and great expectation was in the air. My parents had spoken to hers and we had agreed that we would get married after the baby was born.

Half way through the sixth month of pregnancy the trouble started. Marva started having these intense pains in her stomach and nightmares at night. She would scream out in the middle of sleep and lash out at unseen phantoms. I would wake her, hold her tight, and talk soothingly to her as she related those horrible dreams to me. We kept it to ourselves, hoping that it would soon pass. However, at the seventh month, she got worse. She would throw up all the time. She complained to me that she felt that things were crawling in her stomach, which had ballooned in size. By now, both our parents could sense something was wrong and we took her to see the doctor.

That day of the 6th of July 1992 will always stand out in my mind as a testament to the unknown and supernatural. The doctors ran test after test and could not find anything wrong. They said it could be stress-related symptoms, that some rest and a soak at the beach would help. Then another doctor asked if she had taken an ultrasound and we replied "no." We had decided that we did not want to know what sex the baby was, however with all these new complications we changed our minds. I wish I could have taken it back.

While they hooked her up to the machine, her father suggested that with such a big stomach like hers it must be twins. All were inclined to believe; even the doctor said he would not be surprised. But surprised was an understatement for what happened next. The ultra sound found no baby. The doctor left the room and returned with three other doctors and they looked and sounded, but no baby could be found in her stomach.

"You're not pregnant," said Doctor Tom. "I have never seen anything like this in all my life," he continued. Marva and the women started crying while we men stood speechless.

"But I can feel things crawling in my stomach every day," sobbed Marva. My heart ached at her pain. I went over to caress her. I rubbed her head and told her how much I loved her. At the same time, I was trying to make sense of the situation, but my mind was numb. Looking around at the faces in the room, I could tell I was not alone.

We took her home the next day, for the doctors could not make anything of it, except to say it was a phantom pregnancy and was caused psychologically as a great desire to have a baby.

Marva complained to me about the pains and the frogs and snakes she kept dreaming about. It so happened that our housekeeper overheard our conversation and told us that she knew of a lady that could help Marva. At this point, we were willing to try anything. She told us that she would go to see the lady later that day to make arrangements.

The next morning, the housekeeper came and told us that the lady said that we should come that day at 3 p.m. At two o' clock, we loaded poor Marva into the car and drove to Tivoli to meet Mama Suki. Mama Suki lived in a little green and white wooden house at the back of a banana field. She was a short and thin-looking woman who wore a large red dress that was a size or two bigger than her. However, she had a warm and friendly smile. Greeting us, she asked us to bring Marva into the house quickly. As soon as she saw Marva, her smile quickly vanished and her eyes darkened, while her forehead wrinkled into a deep frown.

"This is worse than I thought," she murmured. Mama Suki ushered us into her bedroom and had us place Marva on the bed. She busied herself gathering herbs, candles, and what appeared to be other esoteric objects.

Marva, in the meantime, was moaning as if she was going into labor. Sweat was streaming down her forehead and body. Her breathing was heavily labored.

When all was ready, Mama Suki asked all to leave the room except for me. Now I don't know what frightened me more, Mama Suki's ceremony or Marva's condition, but I was scared shitless. Closing the curtains, she lit two black candles; two frankincense incense were lit too. She then turned to me and warned me, whatever was to happen next, do not speak.

Mama Suki then began her incantations. They were long. She whipped herself into a frenzy, her eyes rolled back in her head, her body shook. Then she became still. Turning to a little cupboard, she appeared to be listening to something or someone, but I could hear nothing. She then walked over to Marva and threw what appeared to be a blue powder in her face and at the same time squeezed open Marva's mouth and poured a vial of some strange concoction down her throat. Convolutions immediately ripped through Marva. Her stomach rose and fell as swells in the sea. She cried out in agony. Mama Suki opened her dress to reveal her stomach, then she painted some mystical looking symbols on it. This set off a pushing out of the stomach as if to bust it.

Marva cried out, "It's coming out, it's coming out!"

"Push, push," responded Mama Suki. Marva, God bless her soul, pushed with all her might and out popped, a big wrinkled Crapo (Frog) with yellow eyes. It just sat there covered in slime. This was the biggest and ugliest frog I had ever seen. Now seeing this transpire in front of me, fright seized whatever little strength I had left, my knees gave out, and I collapsed onto the floor, pissing myself in the course.

Mama Suki took the frog and placed it into a black box and then uttered some strange words, shook the box three times, and cast the frog out the window. "Your woman is okay now; her stomach will return to normal in three days. It's was a good

69

thing you brought her here today, for if nine months had elapsed, she would be dead!" stated Mama Suki. "Now, the spirit told me that the frog was placed in Marva through Obeah, by her friend Roxanne, who went all the way to Guyana to bring about this mischief." Now I have sent the frog back to who sent it, for it must have a place to stay or a host. Since it cannot cross the sea to Guyana, then it will find the one who paid for it to enter Marva and lodge itself with a vengeance in her." "What duh-duh I owe you?" I stammered. "Nothing. I hate evil and I work for blessings and not money," she replied humbly. Thanking her, we left her house, never again to return. We never told our parents what happened inside, except to say that Mama Suki had prayed and gave Marva a spiritual cleanse.

Three days later, Marva's stomach returned to normal without a stretch mark. A month later, we went off to school in the UK. Marva went on to become a doctor and I chose to be a writer. We now have two beautiful children; Ava, five years and David, seven years old. However, we have never returned to Grenada since, but we do plan to go this summer.

Oh, you must be wondering what became of Roxanne. Well, the last I heard was, she has been pregnant now for the last 17 years.

Fame

"Dust to dust, ashes to ashes, amen," said Father Romeo, making the sign of the cross at the same time, bringing the burial ceremony to its conclusion.

As the dirt fell on the coffin, it made a duh-duh-duh sound. I could not help but muse that this was to be the final sound ever to come from that hole again.

"Woii, oh God, no, no, not him," wailed his sister. Crying erupted all over Cemetery Hill Burial Ground. The sound of her tormented cry made my soul ache. I reached out, pulled her into my arms, and held her as she buried her head into my bosom. Her body shook with spasms while her sobs were muffled on my chest. I could only imagine her pain, so I held my peace. *What can I say to change her grief? Where does her pain begin? Where does it end?* I thought. The best thing I could do for her was to stand by her silently as nature ran its course.

I am not a sentimental man by nature, but my eyes did well up with tears. The atmosphere was thick with emotions. Looking around me, I could see thousands of people. It felt like the entire island had come out. Yet I would not be surprised if they did, for the man lying in the hole was not only my best friend, but the greatest Soca star ever to take the stage.

I am talking about the one and only "Fame!" From Grenada to New York, to London, his music played at all Caribbean parties, especially his newest hit, "I Can't Whine but Ah Could Juk!" Everybody knew that song by heart; school children, their parents, and even their grandparents. Fame had won the Soca Monarch ten times in a row. His songs always seemed to resonate with you.

In the last ten years, he had built a soca empire, but his reign was short lived. You see, Fame had a dark secret, one which he only divulged to me six weeks before he passed, begging me to keep his secret. The problem is that I am not good at keeping

71

them. Can I trust you, the reader, to stay silent? You promise not to say a word?

Fame was born in Snell Hall in St. Patricks, Grenada. He was the first of two children. His sister Betty was born two years later. His father was a calypsonian and had won the crown four times, while his mother taught music at Mc Donald College. So, with this in mind, you might assume it safe to say that Fame would be musically talented. You would be wrong! Fame had an okay singing voice for the shower. He could not play any musical instruments, even though he tried his best. But Fame loved music. He had once told me, that the first time he saw his father singing on the stage and the crowd dancing to his beat, he knew then and there, although he was only ten, that he too would be a calypsonian.

Every day, he would practice singing whatever was the latest soca or calypso hits. His father and mother listen from inside the house as he murdered song after song. They would quietly whisper, "How far the apple has fallen from the tree?" and would laugh quietly. They loved their son, but knew he was not cut out for music. They tried to suggest other disciplines indirectly, but they were lost on him.

There was one person, however, who took notice and admired Fame's persistence and spirit. Papa Pierce would stand and listen while nodding his head as if to imply or convey to Fame that he was digging his vibe. Fame was thrilled by his audience of one.

Fame entered the junior soca monarch when he was 13 years old and placed last. He entered every year until he was eighteen and never moved up from last place, but Fame kept writing songs and believing that one day his time would come.

That day proved to be his eighteenth birthday. He was under the mango tree in his yard composing a song when he felt the presence of someone. Looking up, he saw Papa Pierce over him, smiling.

"Papa P, wha' going on?" asked Fame.

"The spirits are happy; so I am too," replied Papa Pierce. Fame smiled at his reply and, returning his gaze to his composition, said, "I could do with the help of one of dem spirit yuh talk about deh, ah matter a fact, I need about six of dem to write a song or two for meh." said Fame jestingly.

"The spirit is always willing if you are willing," replied Papa Pierce seriously. The change of tone was not lost on Fame. Turning back to Papa P, he looked him in the eyes for a second or two. He noticed for the first time how forceful Papa P's eyes appeared; steady and dark. He sensed a subtle power emanating from them, which caused him to twitch. Papa Pierce broke out into a smile, which Fame returned nervously too.

"Fame, what would you do or give to be the greatest soca artist?" asked Papa P.

"Anything and everything," replied Fame without a thought.

"I am serious, Fame," stated Papa P ominously.

"Do you see any skin teeth?" returned Fame.

"I am going to help you, Fame, but you will have to sell your soul and in return Tall Man will tune your voice."

Fame closed his eyes. He imagined all the glory, excitement, money and, yes ironically, fame that would be his, for such a lousy thing as a soul. A thing, he wondered, what use it was to him now, so what if he exchanged it for something he could touch? Had he opened his eyes, he would have seen the most sinister of grins on Papa P's face.

Two minutes later, he opened them. Papa P's grin was long gone. "I am willing to make the deal," he bluntly stated.

"Good, in five days, come and see me at my house," said Papa P. With that, he got up and walked in the direction of his home.

Five days later, Fame found himself standing in front of a little unpainted wooden house that sat on four stilts. Their wood was grey and black from the beating of Mother Nature, yet they appeared sturdy. The house had one door and two windows. In the yard, there were colored flags everywhere. A mango tree stood to the right of the little tidy yard and there appeared to be three ripe Calivigny mangos on them. A coconut tree and a papaya tree swayed in the breeze to the left of the house, while their branches cast shadows in the huge copper of water under them. The door was a split top and bottom design. One could open the top and keep the bottom closed or vice versa.

"Fame, come, come inside, man," came Papa P's voice from the house. Fame entered the house up three little steps. The inside was sparsely furnished. There were two chairs, a table, a little kerosene stove, a radio, a tiny cabinet, and a bed behind a bamboo curtain.

"Sit down, man, everything good," said Papa P in the same breath.

"Yes, Papa P, the man just eerie."

"Now, Fame, what I am about to tell you, you cannot share with anyone, not even your own mother; do you understand? Fame nodded in agreement. "In this black bag, there is a special stone. Take it out," ordered Papa P. Fame took it out. It was smooth and brown with black swirls about it. It was about the size of a quarter and weighed four to five grams.

"Take this stone and bury it at any crossroad on Thursday between the hours of 12 a.m. to 3 a.m. Do not let anyone see you and do not look back. Three days later, return to the spot around the same time. A tall black man in a suit will come up to you and return the stone you did bury days before. You and him will come to an agreement. However, do all that he says and honor your word and your dreams would be realized."

Thursday at 12 a.m., Fame carried out Papa P's instructions to the letter.

Three days later, on a Sunday, he returned to the spot around 2 a.m. The night was dark, for it was cloudy and it had rained earlier. The air was cool, the road wet, and all was quiet. No one was about; not one dog barked as he made his way to the crossroads. It took him about ten minutes to get there.

Arriving, he looked about him for the stranger that was to meet him. Not a soul was in sight. Half an hour passed, nothing. Forty-five minutes, still nothing. Looking at his watch, he decided to give the stranger until three o'clock, for he figured that he, Fame, must have came later and the stranger had already come and gone... His thought was suddenly broken; galloping sound and the strained breathing of an animal shattered the stillness of the night. He spun around startled, only to make out a large white horse bearing down on him. He leaped backwards to get out of the way. The horse came to a stop a foot away from him. Its eyes were fiery red in the darkness. A tall man sat on its back in a suit that belonged in a museum. Fame could hardly breathe; his legs were frozen and a helplessness swept over him.

Fame could not remember the stranger dismounting, but the next thing he knew, the stranger was standing next to him. "Fame, here is the stone you buried. I have blessed it. Guard it with your life, never have sex with it on you or it will leave you and I will come and take your soul. Every day, place it in a cup with warm water and a tablespoon of honey and drink the water. It will tune your voice and all who hear you will be captivated. If all goes well, I will come for you in twenty years from tonight." Poor Fame could only nod in agreement or was it acknowledgement? Who could tell under such duress?

With that, the stranger placed the stone in Fame's hand and vanished. The stone was hot and seemed to stick to his hand. He could not tell if his mind was playing tricks on him, but he felt a pulsing emitting from it.

Placing it in his pocket, he headed home.

Three months later, Fame released his first hit, "Bigger Is Better," followed by, "Two Gal Not Enough." Fame's voice was captivating; the beat of his songs seemed to weave a spell over his audience. The strangest thing is no one seemed to remember that a couple of months ago, he could hardly sing. Fame went on the win competition after competition. His music was everywhere on everyone's lips.

Ten years went by quickly, and in those years, I started dating his sister and we somehow became best friends. So six weeks ago, while drinking, he narrated his tale to me. He admitted to me that the only reason he told me at all was because he knew his time was over. Fame had lost the stone. He had always been careful, but after winning his tenth Soca Monarch title, he had sex with one of his back-up dancers, and he had forgotten to put away the stone. The next day, he searched high and low, but to no avail; the stone was gone. He also told me at night he would hear a horse trotting under his bedroom window. Sleep was hard to come by for him; he

75

wanted me to stay up and play video games all night with him. I tried to tell him that was just a bunch of crap; he was over exerting himself with all the performances and alcohol consumption. That a vacation would help clear his mind. However, he would have none of it, and insisted that what he told me was the God's truth. He made me promise to look after his sister when he was gone and never to dabble in Obeah. I promised half heartedly, not expecting anything to come of it.

But here I am, six weeks later, holding his sister and looking down on his grave; Fame died after choking on a smooth brown stone with black swirls around it while having dinner; How it got there, no one knows.

Fame's sister had stopped sobbing, having exhausted her tears reservoir. Taking her hand, we headed out of the cemetery. At the top of the hill, we turned to look one last time at Fame's resting place. There, standing next to the grave, was a tall dark man in a suit that belonged in a museum.

The English Lady and the Woodman

For the first time, I am about to reveal what caused me to stop drinking alcohol. You see, I am still trying to make sense of what happened three years ago, so this is more of a plea for help than a story.

Maybe one of you, my audience, can figure it out, for God knows how hard I have tried since that fateful night.

It all happened on a Monday night too.

You could feel the pulse from miles away. The roads were bustling with activity as cars, trucks, and people navigated its meanders; most of the movement in the direction of the city. One could tell this night would know no peace or quietness.

I disembarked the bus to loud, blaring music that seemed to come from all directions at the same time. There was smoke drifting in the air and tonight there were to be no spice fragrances riding her currents, but in its place, BBQ pork, cigarette smoke, and Ganga.

All about me, people were shoulder to shoulder; women and men were dressed in t shirts with jeans, others in skirts and shorts. Everyone had a drink or two in their hand. "Woii, woii, woii, it must be carnival!"

Monday night mass it was. I made my way over to the carnival to meet up with my friends, who were to wait for me by the fire station. I could not help but notice all the sexy ladies just chipping by...yes, tonight was going to be a good night. Before I left home, I had done my stretches and my waist was feeling loose. It was ready for any whiner gal tonight.

I made my way through Sendal Tunnel to the library, making a left at the waterfront. There were a myriad of lights bouncing off the water. Tonight, there would be no sleep for fish or   man.

As I walked pass the Nutmeg Restaurant, I happened to glance left; our eyes met, I felt as if someone had pushed me. I froze in my tracks. Standing in the back of a few revelers was a gorgeous woman. She wore a smile that could light up any room. My pulse was racing. Now, I kinda figure myself to be a ladies man, so I decided to try my luck. So, I crossed the street and made my way to her, our eyes never straying once.

"Hello, are you waiting for someone?" I asked coyly.

"Maybe yes or maybe not," she replied just as coyly.

"Are you from the UK?" I asked after hearing her accent.

"How could you tell?" she teased. I looked her up and down. She was fine. Boy, was I liking what I saw. The long white skirt hugged her long thighs, while a white t-shirt with one end tied, exposing her navel, sent my blood pressure up.

An a English JCB (just come back) too. Woii, I was going to hit that in every which way tonight. I thought. She smiled sweetly that moment at me too.

Anyway, to cut a story short, we decided to walk over to find my friends at the fire station. On the way, she told me she was on holiday for two weeks, that her mother was from St. Davids and her dad from London. She was twenty-five and was a student at the London School of Economics. I found it so easy to talk to her too. When she listened, it was like her whole body did. She would lean in while nodding her head in acknowledgement or in accord with my story. I found her so refreshing; her accent did prejudice my judgment too.

Arriving at the Fire Station, I could not find my friends. Anyway, I was praying not to. Taking her hand, I maneuvered us through the crowd to a bar tent and ordered two rum and cokes. That was followed by six more; the DJ then threw on Tall Pree's song "Old Woman Alone Ah Taking Home." With my drink in one hand and the other around her waist, we started moving to the beat. With the rum in my head, the hypnotic rhythm of the music, the lights, and her sexy body rubbing up against me, I wanted to take her right then and there. All the blood rushed down into the snake and he jumped up, till he was standing straight as the lamppost across the street.

Feeling it, she turned slightly and gave me a sly smile. Then she pushed back against it hard. From there, it was all a blur. I remember dancing and drinking some more. We had even jump up in a band or two. When it was over, she turned and kissed me. Taking my hand, she led me to a bus that was running to St. Davids.

I never felt so hot for anyone before. I could hardly contain myself. The bus left town and soon we were dashing through whatever was left of the night. On an empty stretch, she stopped the bus. We got off and paid the conductor, who had a bewildered expression on his face, but he said nothing.

When the bus moved off, we were left in darkness. "Where is your house?" I drunkenly asked,

"It's up that gap; come follow me," she replied. So I followed her up a trail that ran next to a little stream and soon came upon a house.

Entering it, I could not see a foot in front of me. "Where are the lights?" I asked.

"Shhh. I don't want to wake anyone," she whispered. So we tiptoed into her bedroom. Pushing me down on the bed, she fell on me and started kissing me all over. She stripped me and herself in the process. Her mouth knew no bounds; her touch awakened every nerve in my body. We made love over and over again. She gave some high whines, some low whines, some back whines. Whatever little sense I had left vanished.

I remember crying out, "Oh God it sweet wee, oh gosh yuh bound to do ah man dhat. Look, take mi bank card, take mi wallet, just doh leave mi." The more I cried out in pleasure the more she whined. Explosion and after explosion ripped through my body. Then I passed out.

The next morning, I got up to the sound of creaking wood as it rubbed against each other. There was a cool breeze blowing against my body and I could hear water flowing in a creek. The bed felt rather hard though, opening my eyes I looked up to see branches over me. "WHAT THE HELL!" I exclaimed, at the same time jumping up. I looked around, bewildered. I found myself standing naked in the middle of a giant bamboo stool. The house was gone and so was the English lady. My clothes lay neatly folded against a rock. With my sudden jump, I felt a pull on my privates. Looking down at it, I saw that it was encased in a bamboo joint. I pulled it out with much discomfort, threw on my clothes, and hightailed it out of there.

79

At the road, there were no houses in sight. I checked for my wallet. It was gone, along with my bank card. At the same time, a car came round the corner and I flagged down a ride.

"What are you doing all the way out here by yourself?" the driver asked. "Yuh en 'fraid La Diablesse take yuh," he joked. All I could do was close my eyes and smile, trying to make sense of what transpired last night.

He dropped me off in town and I made my way home.

Arriving home, I met my brother and his friends in the yard, relaxing under the mango tree. Upon seeing me, they cheered, "Look the woodman; last night we see yuh wid ah English woman; come tell us what happen."

"We know yuh mash up that thing."

I stood still for a moment as questions flew at me from all directions. It all came crashing back to me. The night, the woman. Everything. A great fear arose in me and I fell to the ground sobbing uncontrollably, I cried and cried; my brother and his friends stood speechless. Getting up from the ground, I walked over to my brother and hugged him, then walked inside to my bed and cried some more. What I was crying about I could not tell. Maybe because I was alive after spending a night with a La Diablesse or maybe because I lost the greatest lover I ever knew or did I lose my mind? What the hell was in that rum?

Outside in the yard, I heard my brother's friend telling him," I never knew woodmen had ah heart."

The Puppy

It was a beautiful Sunday night. I had gone to the Anglican Church Annual Harvest and Dance. It had gone really well. I even attended the tea party earlier that afternoon, where I dined on pastries and sipped on green tea, while looking at the ladies parading about in their hats and colorful dresses.

I tried my hand at the various games, and I ended up winning a watch at the punch board game. However, the real action began after sunset, when the DJ turned it up. People from all over the island came. It was a festive time.

That night I danced away to soca , reggae, and dance hall music. The girl I had met and befriended at the bar turned out to be quite a dancer. Boy, ah telling yuh. We wound down to the ground and back up again and again; we wound with one foot in the air, against the wall, all that with my Guiness Stout still in my hand. The party ended at midnight.

I asked my dance partner how she was getting home. She told me that she lived only a half mile away and that she would walk it. I myself lived in the opposite direction. Being the gentleman rogue that I am, I offered to walk her home, hoping to get a kiss for my troubles. The moon was bright and big in the sky, not a single cloud was in sight.

We walked along the road, chatting away, hand in hand. The cool morning air blew against us gently. The trees cast shadows as they swayed to and fro. It was so bright that we could see clearly across the valley, and the moonlight even reflected brightly off the unpainted tin roofs of houses, illuminating whatever trees were in its path.

We talked about school, parents, plans for the holidays, which friends we had in common, and when we would see each other again. We rounded a corner that was not so brightly lit, for a huge Hog Plum tree obscured the moon light from reaching the road. I looked around quickly and, seeing no one around, I pulled her to me and brushed my lips against hers. She responded by parting her lips and the kiss deepened. It lasted an eternity. When I opened my eyes, a little white puppy was standing ten feet away, looking at us.

Now that might not be a strange thing, for dogs are common about the island, but there was something different about this one. It just stood there without a sound and stared fixedly at us. It have me chills. My friend, sensing something, turned to see what caught my attention. She shuddered at the sight of the puppy, which looked about six weeks old. "Let's go," she said, pulling my hand. So we started walking. I looked back and the puppy was gone. "That puppy gave me the creeps," she said.

"Me too, did you see how it just sat there?" I replied. She shuddered again.

A hundred meters up the road, we saw a white puppy sitting under a banana tree. This puppy look like it was about six months old. What was odd, it seemed to be the same puppy that we saw earlier. Its actions were the same and it gave off a negative vibe. My friend squeezed my hand tightly and we hurried pass the dog.

"How much further?" I asked nervously.

"Three more corners and we will be there," she whispered. So, picking up the pace, we continued.

Around the next corner, we came face to face with the white dog. This time it was fully grown and in the middle of the road. My friend jumped behind me while gasping out, "Oh God, what is this?" I was so scared that I could barely move. I decided to pass to the left side of the dog. It moved left too. I tried right, it moved right. My friend started crying and I started shaking. Turning around to head back up the street, we found the big white dog there too. No matter what direction we turned, it was there. We screamed, but not a sound came out of our mouths. The dog then began to grow bigger and bigger right before our eyes. It grew to the size of a donkey. It then started to approach us. The two of us peed ourselves right then and there.

At the same time a car came round the corner, the dog vanished. The car came to an abrupt stop, for we were in the middle of the street. "Sancho, yuh trying to get yourself killed?" shouted the driver. It turned out to be my uncle. We ran to the car, jumping in. We related our tale breathlessly. My friend started crying again. My uncle told us that we were lucky, that the dog would have harmed us. That it was an Obeah man or woman who was looking to sell a soul to the devil. We dropped my friend off and I promised to call the next day. She hurried into her house as quickly as she could. My uncle then dropped me off at home. Sleep was hard to come by, and with the light on in my room too.

The next morning, my mom sent me to the shop to buy a pack of Crixs and a tin of Vienna sausages for breakfast. Walking out to the road, I ran across Miss Letty, who upon seeing me, said, "Little boys must not kiss girls under Hog Plum trees late at night or else puppies might bite." She then hobbled off down the road.

The Hunter

Toby was Grenada's version of Tarzan. His parents were Rastafarian and they had gone to live in the mountains, returning as they said to God's way. So, it was during their sojourn in the forest, Toby was born. Five years later, they returned to society, abandoning their way of life; for it had become too hard on them and they missed the company of others. Toby, by this time, knew nothing else but this life.

This was home; he would run between the bushes, leap over fallen logs, and skip over river stones in crossing. His world was one of wonder and intrigue; he knew the different choruses of the birds, where to find the biggest crayfish, where armadillos lived, and the coming and going of possums. He could smell the fragrance of ripened bananas from a mile away. Toby could even tell the subtle difference in taste of water from the various springs in the region.

To Toby, the forest had a pulse and he could feel its beat. So it was depressing to him when he was taken to live among society. He was forced to attend school, to learn to read and write, to add and subtract numbers. Why did he need these things? he wondered. What use was there to him in the forest? He loved living in the moment. With all this said, Toby excelled in school to the point where he had to be skipped to a higher grade. The teachers were at a loss for his brilliance. Maybe being born in the forest and not being bombarded by the fears and negative energy of villagers and society gave him a clean slate to start from. Whatever it was, Toby's future looked bright.

Toby grew up in the capital. Every summer vacation, he would spend with his grandma in the country. These were the happiest days of his life. He and his friends ran wildly through the forest; none could keep up with him. Toby ran barefoot too. He loved to feel the mud between his toes. They would swing from tree to tree on vines that hung from the canopy of the forest. When they were bored of doing that, they would go in

85

search of mangoes, oranges, and coconut water. Being sated, they would take the branch of a palm tree and slide down whatever hill looked smooth; tearing and putting holes in their pants. After that, it was on to the river for a quick swim and then homeward before the sunset.

It was during one of these summer holidays that Toby decided to go hunting with his uncle, who was a renowned hunter. Toby never liked to hurt animals for he was a vegetarian; but he understood that everyone was not alike in taste. He went along, only because of his love for being in the forest. His uncle, on the other hand, made his living from hunting and was quite adept at it too.

The moon was full as they made their way through the forest. Toby held the crocus bag and the machete, while his uncle held the flashlight and banganet; three hunting dogs lead the way. Toby did not need any flashlight for his eyes seemed to take in everything and after five or so minutes, he was in tune with the pulse of the forest.

Half an hour later his uncle's beam rested on two red eyes on a tree in the distance. Toby quickly realized that was not a possum, but a serpent. Coming closer to the tree, they soon confirmed Toby's suspicion. His uncle looked at him and smiled. This boy never ceased to amaze him in the forest. Illuminating the serpent fully, they saw that it had a rat in its mouth. It was a huge red serpent too; Toby reckoned it to be eight feet long. They moved on.

Coming down the hill to the big silk cotton tree, Toby suddenly felt a sense of dread sweep over him. It weighed so heavily upon him that he stopped in his tracks for a split second or two; at the same time, the dogs growled lowly more in fear than in excitement. This was not lost on his uncle, who stopped and swept his beam around. Seeing nothing, he continued downhill. Toby shook off the feeling and followed. "Ah ha, look, Toby, there he is," whispered the uncle, at the same time illuminating a huge possum in a branch of the silk cotton tree. This was the biggest possum they both agreed that they ever saw. The strange thing was that the dogs did not react as they would under normal circumstances, by running up to the tree and barking nonstop. Neither of them noticed, for they were in awe at the size of the possum. Uncle was thinking a catch like this would cement his legend. Toby, thought his eyes were playing tricks on him. The dogs were thinking, *Where are the possums?*

Creeping up on the tree with the lights off to position themselves better, they realized that under the tree was clean from shrubs and was perfect for the catch. There was nowhere for the possum to run. Tonight hunting history would be made.

Do you guys think that I should continue this tale? I am a bit hungry and I can smell the Christmas cake in the oven. What? You don't care? Oh, you would like a piece and some sorrel. Sure, it's Xmas. Come on over. Okay. Where were we, ah yes. Let's return to Toby and Uncle.

In position under the possum, Uncle hit the light and illuminated it. The possum just sat there; it was bigger than they had imagined. It was whitish, with a big head and a shorter tail than usual. The dogs went crazy. They started barking and pawing the tree. Uncle handed the flashlight to Toby to keep it trained on the possum's eyes, while he prepared to spear it with the banganet. In all this excitement, the possum just sat there; the sense of dread returned to Toby. Uncle thrust the spear at the possum; it went straight through it like it was air. Uncle lined up and thrust again, with the same result." What the hell!" cried Uncle. On the third attempt, he hit the branch and the possum fell. *Bup, bup duh bup!* Uncle was so worked up by now he shouted, "Toby, quick, shine the light on it." Toby did and the possum was in the middle of the dogs; however, the dogs seemed not to notice and they just sat there. Uncle, seeing this, dived at the possum, only to fall in thin air.

Toby was holding the light and saw his uncle fall on top of the possum, yet the possum reappeared a foot away from where Uncle had landed. Toby started trembling. Uncle was going crazy; he looked to his left and saw it. He dived after it again and again with the same result.

Still, the dogs were oblivious to the possum. Uncle was now in a frenzy; the possum took off down the track. Uncle snatched the flashlight from Toby's frozen hands and took off after the possum. Toby could not move; he cried out to his uncle to come back but it was useless. The look he had seen on his uncle's face was one of possession. Suddenly, he heard his uncle give a blood curdling scream and then a thud! Then an eerie laughter pierced the night. This proved too much for Toby; he took off homebound. Skipping through bushes, leaping drains and logs, he made it home, pounding on the door, screaming for help. This commotion awoke the neighbors, who inquired what was wrong. Toby had to repeat his story three times because he was hysterical. The men quickly grabbed their flashlights, machetes, and one a gun. With Toby leading the way, they soon came upon the dogs barking. Following the barking, they found the dogs on the edge of a cliff. Approaching the cliff all were struck with a sense of dread, for they could sense the outcome. And sure enough, at the bottom on a pile of rocks, lay the lifeless body of Uncle.

Next to him, lapping up his blood, was the biggest possum any villager had ever laid eyes on. Not a whisper left any man's lip. Toby knew what he was witnessing was the supernatural and the forest was not as tranquil as he had once imagined. He knew he would never return after that night; looking at his uncle's lifeless mangled body, he could not help but muse how the great hunter had become the hunted.

Lilly, the Lady of the River

It was a cold and foggy evening in Acton, which lies in west London. As I exited the Redback Tavern, I was met by a strong gust of cold air that sent shivers throughout my body. Pushing my hands into my pockets and lowering my chin to my chest to protect my neck, I made my way home.

My modest house soon came into view. It was illuminated throughout. This could only mean my daughter and my grandchildren were there. "Oh my, yes, I had forgotten that I had promised to baby sit," I thought out loud. Picking up my pace, I hurried home.

"Grandpa, Grandpa!" shouted Dale and Sam as they hurled themselves into my arms. This show of affection quickly warmed my chilled body and I soon forgot about the nasty weather outside. My daughter came over to greet me; she told me she had to run and we would talk later. With that, she was out the door into the dark foggy night.

Taking my coat off, I walked over to join my grandkids in the living room to sit around the fireplace. I loved to stare into the fire; it reminded me of my beloved country of birth five thousand miles away. Ah yes, I am referring to the Isle of Spice, Grenada. The crackling sound of the wood reminded me of the tastiest food I have ever eaten, flavored with the smoke of the burning wood. Yes, the stew chicken and dumplings, green banana, and sweet potatoes. Mmmhm. To this day, the memory was so strong that the taste of the food arose in my mouth.

"Grandpa, can you tell us one of your scary stories from Grenada?" begged Dale.

"Yes, yes," chipped in Sam.

Closing my eyes, I remembered an encounter I had with a lady many moons ago. Taking a deep breath and releasing it in an exaggerated manner, I began my narration.

"I was only a boy of sixteen then. Our house was only a stone's throw from the river. So you can only imagine, I learned to swim at the early age of four and fished for crayfish and

89

mullet by six. My friends and I would swing from vines on trees that towered over the river basin and leaped into the middle of the pool. Yes, children, those were the good and innocent days of my life.

It so happened one evening that I was up in a mango tree, sucking a Calivigny, when a sudden movement caught my eyes to the right. Sitting on a rock was a beautiful girl around my age. She was combing her hair, which fell about her shoulders. The water beaded over her body while capturing the light of the sun, turning them temporarily into diamonds. She wore the most beautiful smile I ever saw. I also noticed that she was half naked. I could not see her feet for they remained submerged.

Sensing something, she looked up and our eyes met. I froze for a moment. She smiled and motioned for me to come down. I dismounted the tree quickly and walked towards her. Her smile widened as I approached her. "Hello, what's your name," she inquired in a sweet voice, which sounded as if she was singing.

"I am good," said I rather nervously.

"Do you come here often?" she asked.

"Yes, every day, I love the river," said I.

"Maybe you should make it your home," she stated.

"If only I was a fish," I replied, laughing.

We talked and talked; she told me that she lived with her mother and grandma. That they had just moved to the area and that she had noticed me before and she was so happy to have made my acquaintance. Our conversation was interrupted by the call of my mother. The sun was making its way down and that meant I had to hurry to bring the goats in for the evening and to cut some candle bush for the rabbits. So we said our good-byes and promised to meet the same time next day.

That night, as I lay in bed, I felt so excited I could hardly wait for the morrow to see her again. At school, I asked my friends if they had noticed any new students or neighbors, but none did. I thought that strange, for the village was small and everyone knew everyone's business. The thought of her sweet voice and beautiful face soon swept away whatever little concern I had. After school, I raced home and changed into my little blue shorts. In the kitchen, I found a sugar apple and two sapodillas. I

90

placed them in a bag to take them for my new friend. "John, yuh hear what happen to Spade Foot? Well he went fishing in the river last week and disappeared. What was left of his body was found this morning, there was no blood in it," My mother asked and answered at the same time. "Please be careful," she warned.

Grabbing the little bag, I hurried to meet my friend. On the way, I thought about Spade Foot; he was a nice guy, a great fisherman and hunter. He was only five feet five inches tall, but he wore size thirteen shoes that his broad feet flattened, thus the name.

My friend was waiting for me. I gave her the fruit, which she ate greedily. "It has been so long since I have had these," she said. Today, her lower body was still submerged.

"Do you always bathe naked?" I asked.

"Yes, its feels better," she replied.

I jumped into the water; it was cool and refreshing. This basin was very deep and in the middle, the water appeared black. We swam back and forth, laughing and ducking each other. I have never in my life seen anyone swim like her. She would blow by me as we raced across the basin. I inquired of her as to where she learned to swim so well. Her reply was that she was born in water and all her family before her too. I laughed at her response. "You know, I don't even know your name," stated I.

"My name is Lilly."

As the evening before, my mother's call soon ended our encounter. As I left the water, Lilly came up to me and said," Because you gave me a gift, I too will give you one. Treasure it, for it will bring you unimagined luck." With that, she plucked a strand of her hair and handed it to me. I picked up a small piece of twig and bonded the hair to it. Promising to meet again on the morrow, I turned to leave when I heard a large splash. We both spun around and came face to face with two half naked women. The look on Lilly's face was one of fear. On the ladies' faces was one of amusement.

"John, I have to go; this is my mother and grandma. Please don't come back here ever again. Please, it's for your own good." Tears were welling in her eyes. "Now go."

91

"What's the rush; are you going to introduce us to your friend?" they chorused. They moved towards us slowly, their eyes locked on mine. I felt myself falling into a deep pit. I could not move; a feeling of dread came over me yet I was helpless and rooted to the spot. As they closed the distance, their faces changed into that of reptile-looking creatures with fangs. I tried to scream, but no sound could come out.

Then, all of a sudden, Lilly spun towards them. In doing so, I finally saw the lower portion of her body; instead of a pair of legs was a mono green scaled body part attached to a huge fish fin. She screamed and charged them. That shifted their attention from me, temporarily breaking their spell. I felt my legs and took off running. I heard huge splashing and screaming in the back ground, but I dared not look back.

I opened my eyes, for I had finished narrating my tale. Dale and Sam sat with their mouths open and hands clenched tightly. At the same time, my daughter opened the front door, breaking the suspenseful awe that the tale had triggered. "Is Grandpa telling you guys one of his tall tales again?" she inquired warmly.

"Yes, Mommy," they cried in unison.

"It's bedtime; say goodnight to Grandpa."

"Goodnight, Grandpa and thanks for the story." With that, I walked them to the door. After waving my good-byes, I turned and walked over to a picture on the wall that featured a beautiful woman sitting half naked on a stone next to a river, with her feet submerged. Taking it off the hinge, it revealed a wall safe. Entering the combination, I opened it. It appeared empty. Placing my hands to the back, I found what I was looking for. I pulled my hand out and opened my palm. In it lay a small twig bonded by a single gold hair that belonged to Lilly, the Lady of the River.

It Was All a Dream

The full moon sat still in its heavenly abode, casting its light as a fisherman would his net, as if attempting to snare all that resided below with her silvery light. The crisp air moved casually through the trees and over the river, resulting in a cool and very refreshing breeze.

The sound of frogs croaking; the hooting of an owl, and the random and scattered barking of the village pot hound dogs was not lost on our main character for this story.

Enter, Mr. Dalton.

This beautiful full moon night found Dalton sitting on the top platform of his house steps. His family was already sound asleep. As he sat taking in the sounds and sights of the night, he began to feel the restlessness of his mind begin to quiet down.

His small and modest wooden constructed home sat amid a highly vegetated area. To the back lay a river that was teeming with crayfish. The water was drinkable, for there were no other houses higher up river that might pollute its soft sweet waters.

On the other side of its banks, Dalton cultivated, Dasheen, Calaloo, yams, sweet potato, and Pigeon peas. The soil in this mountainous region was very fertile due to its volcanic composition.

To the front of his house were two acres of flatland. On this, he cultivated bananas, oranges, grapefruit, plantains, sorrel, lettuce, tomatoes, guava, and mangoes. These crops, along with hunting and fishing, made up the sum of his subsistence.

As he sat on the stairs, he chewed slowly on a fried bake, which he had packed with salted codfish, cucumbers, onions, sweet peppers, a little hot sauce, and drizzled lightly with coconut oil. As the taste serenaded his taste buds, the aroma of the hot cocoa tea assaulted his scent glands. I reckon that the

93

combination of the setting, the food, the moon, and the breeze finally brought an end to his racing mind.

Dalton had been worrying about how hard he had to work to support his family and himself. He had two children; Betty, who was eleven years old, and Thomas, who was sixteen. Dalton loved his family very much and prayed for a change in his financial status. There was also his homely wife Gertrude who took care of the children and household without a murmur of dissatisfaction. She was a devout Christian and a very optimistic individual. To say the least, she was content with her lot in life.

Dalton had one other relative; his brother Humphrey. He lived a half mile down the road and operated a grocery and rum shop. Humphrey was very greedy and selfish. He lived his life in a very miserly fashion and always complained of how broke he was.

The two brothers rarely had intercourse and when they did, it was brief. Dalton would drop by the shop to pick up some salted cod, butter, rice etc. They would greet each other cordially and inquire of the other about their health. Humphrey would also send his greetings to Dalton's family. Paying for his items, he would thank his brother and depart.

Dalton loved his brother dearly but learned at an early age not to have any prolonged conversation with him, for it always lead to an argument and ill feelings afterwards. Humphrey always had to be right even though he rarely ever was. This was due to his insecurities.

Swallowing the last of the bake, Dalton washed it down with the cocoa tea that had cooled somewhat due to the constant flow of cool breeze. Standing up, he looked up at the sky and uttered," God if you're up there, yuh see how hard a wuking, please help meh, shower meh wid money." With that, he turned and walked inside, shutting the door.

Enter the Dream:
That night, Dalton slept deeply; his body was so relaxed, his wife's body and the blanket provided the right amount of warmth, while the night wrapped them in darkness, due to the curtains.

As he drifted off into dreamland, he found himself sitting under an old pine tree that stood next to a huge boulder that had strange marking on it. In the dream, he remembered that this pine tree and boulder were on his property. He suddenly felt a presence. Spinning about, he came face to face with his long departed grandpa.

"Dalton, you have worked hard all your life. Tonight, God has heard your prayers and has sent you a gift. However, this gift must be shared equally with your brother Humphrey.

"Tomorrow, you and Humphrey go to the boulder, take up positions on either side of it. Place your hands on it together; the boulder would then begin to vibrate. When this happens, both of you lift the boulder up; it would have become light as a feather. As soon as it is overhead, a copper full of gold and jewelry will come up. Quickly throw in a penny or remove any item from it. Doing so will prevent it from going back down. For it can only rise and fall with exactly what it contained. This money was buried there three hundred years ago by pirates who killed thirteen of their own and buried them together with the treasure. Because of this, the spirits of the dead men have guarded it jealously. Have no fear of this. Do as I have told you and you will be rich as any king. However, you cannot utter a single word of this to anyone nor can you go by yourself," said Grandpa. With that, he departed.

I know you guys can hardly wait for the rest of the story. Maybe I should leave it up to your imagination to finish. What was that? Did you just suck your teeth at me? Huh? All right, all right, if you insist, I will gladly continue.

Enter the Treasure:
Next morning, Dalton arose with a flood of energy, caused by excitement. Looking across at his wife, he smiled. She was still asleep. *Good,* he thought. He did not want her to see him, for she was very intuitive and would sense the change in him. She would then proceed to question him and he could and would not lie to his wife. So, pulling the sheet off him, he tiptoed outside to go pee. Then, after, he would run down to his brother

95

Humphrey and either by persuasion or force, he would bring him back to find the treasure.

Dalton remembered countless tales of people who had dreamed about finding money and did so. Some, he recalled, did not end well. One story he recalled was of a certain Mr. Benny, who dreamed of a copper of money by the river, but in the dream, the spirit told him he would have to give up his only son in exchange for it. The next day, he took his son with him to the spot. The ground started shaking and the copper started rising. Looking at his son's innocent face, he had a change of heart, turned his back on the copper, and walked away. Years later, he mortgaged his lands to send his son to school in the UK. The son took the money and partied and chased women in London instead of attending school. When the news reached him of his son's worthless behavior, he fell down with a stroke. On his dying bed, his last words were, "If I only knew that jackass would ah turn out so and would ah sell he arse for the copper of money; at lease ah would have dead happy." With that, he passed.

Dalton opened his door and was startled to find his brother sitting on his stoop. "Humphrey, wha yuh doing here?"

"Dalton, boy, ah had a dream last night about ah copper of money, but ah to take you with meh to get it," stated Humphrey, at the same time shifting from foot to foot in excitement while rubbing his hands in greedy anticipation.

Placing his forefinger to his lips to signal silence, Dalton pulled his brother down the stairs and out under the mango tree. There, they both related their dreams. They matched word for word, scene by scene. Dalton then went to the outside kitchen, took his cutlass and two fine bags, and they both headed of to find to boulder.

They did not speak to each other the whole time. The giant pine tree soon came into view and soon after the huge boulder. At its sight, they sped towards it.

To say the boulder was huge is to understate its size. The thing was as big as a house. It was black and had moss and plants growing all over it. It looked like it could be the foundation stone that the Earth was built on.

Taking up positions on either side of the boulder, they placed their hands on it together. Suddenly, there was a loud crackling sound that startled both brothers. The boulder began to vibrate. For a moment, Dalton thought that it might dislodge itself from the ground and roll over them. Looking over at Humphrey, he could see his eyes consumed in greed and colored by impatience. As they raised their arms, the boulder lifted off the ground, revealing a hole.

Another vibration ensued, this time from the ground. A copper that could hold five grown men rose slowly. Inside, it was filled with gold and precious stones.

The sight of so much wealth proved too much for Humphrey. "Oh God, woii, look at money," he cried. His greed now was full blown. Why did he have to share this evenly with his brother Dalton. "Dalton, the spirit told me three quarters of this money is mines," lied Humphrey.

"No, it did not say so; it said that it was to be shared equally," replied Dalton angrily.

"Dalton, I am your older brothda, three quarters belong to me!" screamed Humphrey. They went back and forth, arguing. Suddenly, Humphrey let go of the boulder and charged Dalton. They both fell to the ground. They punched and scratched each other, all the while rolling and wrestling. Five minutes later, they lay on their backs, exhausted. Turning to look at each other, Humphrey said, "All right, fifty-fifty."

They both got up and turned towards the boulder. It had lodged itself firmly back into its former position. "Oh no!" they cried in unison as they made a dash for it. Placing their hands on it, they tried to lift it but to no avail. There would be no vibration ever again from that rock.

They both began sobbing, all their dreams of grandeur washed away by their tears in the process.

Twenty minutes or so later when they had exhausted their reservoir of tears, they got up and headed home.

On the way, no one knew what got hold of Dalton. Not even Dalton himself; for he was always a very quiet and gentle person. Seizing his brother by the arm, he started plan-arsing (striking with the flat side of the machete) him with the machete.

"Woii, help, help, murder, murder," cried Humphrey. "Woii, Dalton trying to kill mi, woii, oh God, doh kill mi, please doh kill meh!" screamed Humphrey.

"Hush yuh stupid arse; yuh too stupid, yuh too stupid," replied Dalton as he landed plan-arse after plan-arse on the bottom and back of Humphrey.

Hearing the commotion, his wife Gertrude came running outside with the kids in tow. Seeing Dalton beating his brother, she ran over and pulled the cutlass out of Dalton's hand. He did not resist. Humphrey could barely walk, but he hobbled away crying, but glad to be alive.

Taking Dalton's hand, she asked, "Dalton, what happen? I never seen yuh like this before."

Looking at his lovely wife and kids, then around at his humble home and cultivated land; he released a long breath. Closing his eyes, he felt the anger leave him. Then and there, he realized how wealthy he was to have a loving and faithful wife, beautiful and caring children, and a land that produced bountiful harvests year after year. Opening his eyes, he pulled his wife into his arms and kissed her. "I love yuh," he said.

"Meh too," she replied.

Turning to look down the road, he could make out poor Humphrey limping in the distance. He needed that whupping, he thought; a smile spread across his face. Yes, he had that years in the making.

As they walked up the stoop to the house, his wife looked up at him and again asked, "What was that all about?"

Smiling at his wife, he replied, "It was all a dream."

DRY RIVER — A Preview!

As I lay here looking at the ceiling, memories of my childhood spring to light.

It's July and school is out, so my father sends me to spend the holidays with my mother and family. I am bursting with excitement. I cannot wait to see my brothers, sisters, and cousins and to begin our summer adventures in a place called Dry River.

I awake to the sound of whispers. As my consciousness returns from its nocturnal travels, I am able to distinguish the voices. It's my Grandma and Papa. I reckon it's about 5 a.m. for everything is cloaked in darkness and that is the time Grandma gets up to start breakfast. Wait a minute; it's Saturday too.

I sit up slowly, not trying to wake my cousins. At the same time, a cock crows its salutations to the sun. I take a deep breath and exhale in a yawn. The aroma of spice drifts along with the crisp morning air. I can make out the scent of nutmeg, cocoa, and cloves. I can feel the energy of the arrival of the new day. Everything is shaking off the residue of yesterday in anticipation of today. I make my way over to the window. It's twilight and my eyes are adjusted by now. I see the chickens busying themselves by pecking the dirt in search of breakfast. By now, the birds have joined in the morning's symphony and as if directed by an unseen director nature showcases her masterpiece.

In the house, there is another symphony, one of pots and pans. My attention is back inside as I hear the others waking up. A scent invades my nostrils, one of salt cod and coco tea and my stomach betrays my presence with a grumble. My cousin comes over to the window too. "What we doing today?" is his greeting.

"Let's go down by the river and catch crayfish and then go look for mango," I reply.

"I know where some big Julie mango is too," he states. "Let's go sit on the veranda."

As we sit outside, Mount Saint Catherine rises majestically through the mist and I am captivated by her beauty. The sun changes her garments from mist and fog to green shrubbery right before our eyes and caps her peak with a cloud. Something catches my attention in the corner of my eye; it's the cat chasing a lizard up the grapefruit tree. The tree's trunk is covered in green moss, which gives it an ancient look, however far from the truth. A noise startles me from my observation of the tree to another tree where a troupe of monkeys is chattering away. The dogs are off barking up the tree behind them, breaking the tranquility of the morning.

Everyone is outside now, trying to figure out the source of the commotion. The monkeys soon move on by jumping from tree to tree, or should I say flying from tree to tree for the distance they covered, and time too.

Grandma shouts that breakfast is ready, so we hurry off to wash our faces and brush our teeth. The table is a large old one, been in the family for a long time too. It's made from a hard wood and polished, giving it a deep, dark finish. At the center of the table sits a big bowl of salt cod mixed with peppers, tomatoes, onions, and coconut oil, the other bowl is filled with fried bake and a pot of hot coco tea completes the settings. By now everyone is hungry and as soon as the blessings are made, we all dive in....Everyone is talking, laughing, teasing and eating; yes, the food is like no other for the energy and vibe of the environment and people make all the difference, but then again, it's Saturday and it's the start of my summer adventure in a faraway place called Dry River.

In memory of my grandmother, Claire Ogilivie

About the Author

Greetings to all under the heavens. My name is Clyde Viechweg and I am the author of *Caribbean Twilight; Tales of the Supernatural.*
I love folklore; their preservation and narrating them.
When I am not writing, I am creating fresh and tasty raw juices that are amazing. Yes, my aim is to bring all under heaven together, through one story and one juice at a time.

Made in the USA
Lexington, KY
19 October 2017